Tom Anderson was born in Blackpool in 1947 and has lived in London since the 1960s. *The Last Days of Dad* is his first published work.

THE LAST DAYS OF DAD

Tom Anderson

Published by Tombuktu Books 2018
Copyright © Tom Anderson 2018
All rights reserved.
ISBN 978-1-9999926-0-6

Acknowledgements

Thanks to Faber and Faber Ltd for permission to quote from 'The Love Song of J. Alfred Prufrock' by T.S. Eliot.

Special thanks to Sally Adams for the cover design. http://sallya.jalbum.net/ And Phil Hall for technical support.

To the memory of my mother and father

Contents

Back Home

First she told him the good news. Plumped on the sofa in housecoat and cardigan, hands folded over tummy, slippered feet on a buffet, she began with his father's operation and how good the private hospital had been. Angelic staff, heavenly food, perfect peace - so much better than the Queen Alexandra in town where the ward was a madhouse and that Pakistani doctor had been so rough with him.

'He'll get better now. You wait and see.'

After that she told him about her best friend Ida's retirement. Thirty one years, most of which they'd worked together side by side. How she'd gone along to watch the presentation by Mr Forbes who'd done the same for her the year before. And how pleased they'd all been to see her. Then the bad news...Mrs Lowther's husband dying of cancer in a hospice. Grace Topley's son in court for snatching a lady's handbag - he'd always been trouble. And young Sandra from just around the corner disappearing for months on end and returning home *out here*.

'Out where?' said Will who knew very well what she meant.

'*Pregnant*. Like this!' She moved one of her hands forward to illustrate. 'I barely recognised her. Her hair used to be lovely - it's gone all limp now and her face is all puffed up. They're keeping quiet about who the father is.'

Will pondered the moral implications of this from his slumped position in one of the two armchairs. There was a torpid atmosphere in general in the room. It had something to do with the shades of night gathering outside, the heat emanating from the electric coal fire and the soft light of the reading lamp over the armchair where his father dozed.

'So,' said his mother expectantly. 'What have you been up to?'

'Nothing much.'

'Are you still sharing that flat with what's-his-name?'

'I am, but I'm thinking of buying somewhere my own.'

'You should move back here. You could get a job in the local library service.'

'I work for the National Library, mum. Not any old library.'

1

'Well, there's the Central Reference Library in town. That's a big place.'

'Not big enough. If there are any jobs going, it'll be Buggins' turn. I'm an outsider.'

'You were born and bred here.'

'But I don't live here any more.'

His mother pushed her spectacles higher on her nose and looked away. There was a silence. Will noticed that his father had on the crumpled blue trousers of an old suit that had once been 'Sunday best', worn proudly on their long-ago walks around town. The ragtag look was completed by a mustard coloured zip-up cardigan. A lock of white hair hung over his brow.

'How's Frances? Have you seen her?'

'I've told you before. We broke up last year. She's with a new guy now.'

'That's a shame. She was good for you was Frances. Better than the other one you were with - what was her name?'

Will racked his memory.

'Angela? Jean? Maura?'

'She mucked in did Frances. Remember when you brought her to the British Legion and she played darts with us?'

'It didn't work out.'

His mother sighed and picked up a magazine. It seemed as if the interrogation was over, but just as she was about to start reading, a gleam of light appeared in her eyes and she licked her upper lip.

'That reminds me,' she said. 'Guess who I saw last week.'

Will looked across at her.

'The Man from the Pru,' he said.

'No.'

'Eamonn Andrews. This Is Your Life.'

'Don't be daft.'

He thought for a moment.

'Casper the friendly ghost.'

'No...Barry Garman the friendly ghost!'

Will shifted in the armchair. A silent alarm had gone off on his neural network, somewhere down in the enteric zone.

'Why does thinking about Frances remind you of Barry Garman?'

'Well, it's just thinking about the past. How long is it since we've seen him?'

Will gazed into the tunnel of time.

'Well, I haven't seen him since I was about...fifteen years old. He sat his exams a year ahead of me, then I just didn't see him very often. I think he went somewhere else to do his A levels.'

'You were very close at one time.'

'Hmm, sort of. He didn't really keep up with the times though.'

She put him in the picture.

'I was standing at the bus stop outside St Oswald's when this man walked past. I could see he was looking at me, but there are some funny people about so I didn't take much notice. The next thing I know, he's standing in front of me saying "It's Mrs Faraday, isn't it?". I looked at him and he said "I'm Barry Garman. Remember me?" And then I could *just about* see the likeness. He's changed quite a bit, but then so have you, I suppose.'

'I haven't given him a second's thought since I left home.'

She gave him brief details of the conversation.

'He's not married then?'

'No, he's another one who hasn't got married by the look of it. At least there was no ring on his finger and no mention of it. Anyway he asked after you and I told him you'd be home today and...well, one thing led to another and I gave him our phone number. He said he'd really like to see you again.'

Will sighed.

'Oh God... He *is* a ghost. I'll have nothing in common with him. You know I haven't kept up with people from that far back.'

'That far back? It seems like yesterday to me. Anyway, just see how you get on. It would be nice to have a friend you could meet up with when you come home. Ooh, goodness...'

She nodded at the sun clock over the mantlepiece.

'Look at the time. I'd better wake your dad or he won't sleep tonight.'

She called her husband's name, then leant across and gently shook his knee. He closed his mouth, opened his eyes and sat up rigid in the armchair trying to get his bearings.

'What is it?' he rasped.

'You don't want to sleep too long, Bill. Your programme's on soon.'

3

His father grunted, then rose slowly to his feet and shuffled unsteadily to the door. The thick pile carpet in the hallway muffled his progress, but after a few seconds Will heard the bathroom door bolt sliding shut.

'He's better than he was, you know. Much better. I kept finding him on his hands and knees before the operation. It was wearing me out.'

Will gazed at the corner where his father spent most of the daytime hours. The armchair was covered with a large blanket flattened and creased with the contours of his father's body. On the floor beside it lay a small pile of newspapers, the top one folded open at the Daily Crossword with all clues completed in neat blue script. On the other side, a coffee table supported a variety of objects. A blue-ringed pint mug, a Toby jug stuffed with biros, pencils and elastic bands, a notepad made from sheets of scrap paper stapled together, a penknife, a big rubber, a football coupon, two stacks of library books and a desk calendar with knobs for changing the date.

'Why does he bother with that calendar thing?' said Will. 'I thought one day would be the same as the next when you're retired. You can just live in the eternal present.'

His mother looked up from her magazine and gaped across at the coffee table.

'Well you can easily forget what day of the week it is when you're retired. He likes to know so he can post his pools on time and remember his doctor's appointments.'

Will heard the toilet flush and a pipe clunk, then the door bolt slide back. A few moments later, his father veered across the living room floor again and subsided into his armchair.

'Where's the whatsit?' he gasped, making a squeezing motion with his hand.

His wife found the remote control and turned on the TV. She uncrossed and recrossed her legs, pushed her spectacles higher on her nose again and pulled the cardigan closer around herself. Lurid images flickered across the screen a few feet in front of them.

'It's another ten minutes yet, you know.'

The phone rang next day as Will sat reading in his bedroom. His father was passing through the hallway and picked up the receiver.

'Hello?' he shouted. '*Who?* Will? You want Will?'

Will put his book down and opened the bedroom door just as his father was about to knock.

'Barry somebody. I couldn't catch his last name.'

'This'll be him,' his mother called from the kitchen. The smell of roast chicken was circulating through the bungalow. He picked up the phone but waited for his father to shuffle into the living room before speaking.

'Hello?'

'Hello. Is that Will *Faraway*? It's your old mate Bazza here.'

Will cringed at the schoolboy humour. It seemed at odds with the deep grown-up voice, although that was still endowed with the local accent. He listened as it spoke in cliches of how are you, long time no see and disbelief at the flight of time. He responded sparingly.

'How about meeting up?' the voice went on. 'Be good to see you again and talk about old times.'

'Could do.'

'I was thinking about a pub lunch but d'you know what I'd like to do first?'

'No?'

'Have a walk round the Fields. Broughton Fields. Right at the heart of the old neighbourhood. That'll bring back some memories.'

'Right...'

'We spent so much time there when we were kids.'

'We did.'

'I drove past it a few weeks ago. It's been smartened up in the name of progress, but it's still recognisable.'

'I haven't been there since my parents moved.'

'Well there you are then. How about tomorrow?'

'Erm...*tomorrow?*'

'Well it's a Bank Holiday, so I'm not at work.'

'Erm......okay.'

They finalised the details, exchanged a few more niceties, then hung up. Will put the receiver down quietly and tried to slip back into his bedroom, but the kitchen door swung open behind him.

'Dinner'll be ready in twenty minutes,' said his mother.

'Great. I'm starving.'

She came and stood in his doorway.

'How did it go then?'

5

'Okay. We're meeting tomorrow morning.'

'Oh, that's nice. I knew you'd want to see him really.'

She looked around the room.

'We're still keeping your things for you.'

Will looked around the room too. She meant the cheap guitar that stood in the corner with a layer of grey dust under its strings. The row of paperbacks that spanned his teenage years - Fleming, Sillitoe, Kerouac and others - on the fold-up table. And the old board games and remains of his Meccano set which were piled on top of the wardrobe. There was not much else left from his childhood really, except for the bed that he'd knelt to pray beside once upon a time.

When she'd gone, he went over to the window. On the sill was a framed photograph showing a young mod in tapered trousers, white shirt and floral tie crouched beside Whisky the dog in Auntie Beth's back yard. He would have been fifteen or sixteen and that was about the last time he could remember seeing Barry. He looked through the window. Beyond the unkempt lawn were fences and slender trees, the backs of other houses and rooftops crowned with aerials. And above all that, a procession of little clouds floating with numbing slowness across the suburban sky.

Will took the bus into town that afternoon and wandered through the familiar network of streets. It was Sunday and most of the shops were closed, but people were out and about including some early season holidaymakers. His first call was the old arcade where he stopped before the partitioned windows of the Pet Emporium and watched a brood of black and white puppies roll and tumble in the sawdust. In the next window, fancy mice slept on top of each other in a heap of fur just as they had done in his childhood. He walked on glancing in shop windows and watching the street life until he came to the new pedestrian precinct. Here were stalls and vendors and a busker proclaiming the end of his days as the wild rover. And at the far end, a group of crop-headed youths, one wearing a Union Jack T-shirt, another dressed as a bear, handing out leaflets and selling a newspaper. He kept well away.

On the seafront, he leant against the iron railing and looked down at the beach. The tide was out but the pounding waves had left ruts in the sand and wide shallows of water. Only a few people were down there and the wind blustered against them. He remembered playing tag along the sea's edge with Fran a year or so ago on a calmer day. And playing football here with school mates on one of those last days of term. And carrying sand home for the garden sandbox when he was a little kid with his mother. He turned and looked both ways along the promenade. Victorian edifices, a hotchpotch of modern buildings, carny shacks and strings of unilluminated light bulbs. The whole place looked gaudy and bleak at the same time.

Next day, Will stood between silver birches on the edge of the Fields. The grass before him sloped smoothly down to the football pitches and Barry was right - everywhere was neatly landscaped now with ornamental trees and tarmac paths. Twenty years ago, it had been wild with bracken and dock, dandelions and clover, self-seeded bushes. Crickets and grasshoppers had kept up a summer-long chorus and small boys could crawl native style through the tall grass without being seen. Back then, there were cavities deep enough to be covered with old doors or sheets of corrugated iron and turned into subterranean dens. And the few paths that existed had been made by human feet over time. That was how he remembered it.

He made his way towards a belt of woodland on the far side of the main entrance. This had hidden a little stream known as 'the dyke' and he and his friends had played tracking and hiding games there and dared each other to jump across the limpid water. In spring, they'd built makeshift dams and for a couple of years, he'd caught tadpoles in jam jars and taken them home to see the miraculous growth of frog limbs. Now the woodland shrank as he got nearer and soon revealed itself as a narrow bark-chipped border of shrubs and bushes. Behind it, black railings marked the edge of a new housing development and a single willow tree dipped its branches over the levelled ground.

He checked the time and looked around. A man was watching from the high bank near the changing huts where they'd agreed to meet. Will set off again in that direction. He knew he was under surveillance and looked searchingly left and right as if every aspect of the park was of interest. A little closer, he glanced ahead. The man stood with legs apart, shoulders hunched, hands in the pockets of a dark blue coat. Closer again, he saw a stocky build bulging in front, black hair combed back and a smooth black beard with tell-tale traces of white. And a face that could have been handsome except for flushed cheeks, small guarded eyes and a sourness around the mouth. Who the hell was this? The stranger greeted him.

'Well, you're still just about recognisable. What happened to the specs though?'

The voice was confident and precise.

'I'm a contact lens sufferer now,' Will said as they shook hands.

'Oh right, so we can't call you speccy four-eyes any more? Don't worry, I'm long past all that childish name-calling. But you don't seem to recognise *me*...'

He pulled out a wallet and opened it. A stained finger pointed at the name embossed on a plastic card.

'Oh, it's all right. I'm not doubting you.'

'Here, remember the old Goon Show? Major Bloodnok? *Open your wallet and repeat after me - help yourself.*'

He laughed loudly. Will smiled briefly.

'Anyway, don't worry.' He put the wallet away. 'Your mother didn't know me from Adam either. It's partly the beard' - he stroked it - 'and partly wear and tear.'

Will shrugged.

'Happens to us all'.

'It does. I reached thirty a couple of years ago and you must be in the same boat. Time seems to be speeding up. I've tried to think when we last saw each other but it's lost in the mist.'

'Probably when we were about fifteen.'

'We drifted apart, didn't we?'

'Something like that.'

They stood looking down at the playing fields. There were few people around. Two dog walkers talking to each other, a young mother waiting for a child to catch up and a lone man striding over the football pitches on his way elsewhere.

'There used to be a concrete cricket pitch in the middle there,' said Barry. 'Holes for stumps at each end. Do you remember?'

'Vaguely.'

'Bloody dangerous when we played with a real cricket ball - what with no shin pads or anything.'

Will saw the red ball again, bouncing up at him off the hard surface. The white stitching on the seam. The loud 'chock' as it met the bat and the way his wrists had ached after hitting it a few times...

'Cigarette?' Barry held out the packet.

'No thanks. I've given up.'

'Very commendable.'

He clicked a flame from his lighter and blew out the first little wisp of smoke.

'You can't enjoy any of the old vices these days without somebody saying it's bad for you.'

'Well the medical evidence is clear, so it's up to you,' said Will. 'It's your funeral. Sorry, I shouldn't have said that...'

He glanced across, but Barry seemed unperturbed.

'I've known people who've smoked all their lives without harm. My mother smoked like a chimney but she didn't die of cancer.'

'Yes, my mother told me. I was sorry to hear about that...'

Barry looked around.

'Shall we sit down for a while?'

Will followed him to a nearby bench, already feeling that he'd got in too deep. But what else could he do? You had to pay your respects...

'She just dropped dead one day,' said Barry after they'd settled. 'That's all that happened. Heart attack. I found her on the living room floor when I called round the next evening...' His voice tailed off, then recovered. 'She'd been using this exercise machine that she'd bought - bloody stupid. I knew she had high blood pressure and all that, but it was a shock, I can tell you. S*ixty one...*' He took a long drag on his cigarette.

Will dredged up his best image of her.

'I remember her riding around on that bike with the drop handlebars. You'd never see my mother doing that. She was a real livewire, wasn't she?'

Barry frowned.

'She wore herself out looking after me, Will. That's been part of the problem. She had three different jobs at one time, just to pay the mortgage and the bills and keep us going.'

9

'What happened to your father? I don't remember him at all.'

'My father fucked off when I was in junior school. I doubt whether he ever sent any money. And I've no idea where the bastard is now. Cremated, I hope.'

'Oh, dear.'

Barry laughed.

'We never did get on. Anyway, let's talk about some thing else. *Your* mother. She's a cheery old soul, isn't she? Much the same as I remember. And Mr Faraday, she told me, is retired and looking after his health. And young Master Faraday I gather is still living in the Great Wen...'

'Did she tell you what I do?'

'She neglected to provide that information. Something shady, no doubt.'

'I'm a librarian - well, more of an administrator really. With the National Library...'

'A librarian...' said Barry. The furrows in his brow deepened. 'I should have guessed. You were always a bit of a bookworm.' He blew out a cloud of smoke. 'I only read my school books. You read all sorts of stuff. Back and forth to Broughton library...I said you'd go blind, what with that and the other thing...'

His eyes gleamed with sly mirth.

'Remember? *Did you do it last night?* '

Will gave a weak smile. There was nothing else for it. He would have to talk to protect himself.

'I didn't spend all my time reading books,' he said. 'We played out quite a lot it seems to me. Over there in fact...' He pointed at two white-lined football pitches laid out back to back in the distance. 'They used to take the goalposts up in May, didn't they? We'd use jackets or bags or bikes after that.'

'Aye...and have big arguments about whether a shot was in or out.'

'I remember lying on the grass there on Sunday afternoons in summer - talking, drinking Corona, listening to Alan's transistor radio. He could tell you exactly where every record was in the charts week by week.'

'It was difficult to shut him up...'

'You were the same about football. Those scrapbooks you kept in big green ledgers. Photos, game reports, league tables - all neatly pasted in. Have you still got those?'

Barry nodded.

'I pick one up every now and then and look through it. A lot of the stuff I cut out of Charles Buchan's Football Monthly. Remember that? It takes you back. Footballers were decent human beings then. Ordinary blokes who played the game and won your respect. Remember Tom Finney, the Preston plumber? Seventy six caps for England and he'd still come round and unblock your toilet.'

'They didn't pay him enough, that's why...'

'Well it's gone to the other extreme now. At the top level anyway. Big business rules the roost - all this advertising, sponsorship, million pound players. All the foreigners coming in...There won't be any all-white clubs left in this country soon.'

The silent alarm went off again.

'There've always been foreign players in British teams, Barry. Remember Cheung - the Chinese centre forward we had for a while? And Bill Perry - he was South African. And Trautmann over at Man City. He was a German with an Iron Cross in his pocket but everybody liked him.'

'They were one-offs, Will. Exotics. Back then, British clubs were 99.9% British. Now the blacks and the dagoes are creeping in and with them anything goes. I tell you, football's finished as a sport.'

Will twisted round as casually as he could and pointed to a spot fifty yards away.

'Remember the bonfires we used to build over there? With Alan and the Meredith brothers and Josie and Malcolm? They were huge. People would come and sling their old furniture on them. Doors, chests of drawers. We had to try and guard them against raiding parties. And we always lit them on 5th November - no other date.'

'There used to be three different bonfires on the Fields. One over there, another one over there.' Barry pointed north and east. 'Nowadays there are none. Well I haven't been here but you hardly see them anywhere - except in people's back gardens. They've started this Hallowe'en business now, copying the Yanks. Frightening people on their own doorsteps.'

Will ploughed on.

11

'Anyway, what happened to you? You went away for a while, my mother said.'

Barry laughed.

'Aye, well I was hoping to keep quiet about this but I went to London too. Not by choice...I landed a place at Imperial College to do chemistry and that was that. My mother would've raised merry hell if I'd turned it down.'

'Absolutely.'

'I lived on campus for a while, then found digs in North London - the poorer side of Highgate. That wasn't a bad area, but London as a whole I hated. The sheer size of the place, the time it took to get anywhere, the people. The blacks were everywhere of course, but I didn't feel comfortable with the cockneys either. Too many Jack the Lads.'

'I like it,' said Will. 'I like the size of the place, the fact that you can get lost in it, the massive choice of things to do and places to go. I suppose all the different cultures might take some getting used to...'

'Well it was just one big bloody mishmash to me. How can you have any normal life when there are so many different races living cheek by jowl? In the house I lived in, there was a loud and stupid Dutchman, a Chinaman who didn't speak any English and looked like a runner for the Triads and some bloke and his mistress from *Guyana* who shared their body odour with you. And that was before you hit the streets.'

'Hmm,' said Will.

'I'd have come home after graduation, but my mother was in the throes of moving house so I stayed on for a while. I went to the Labour Exchange - that was an eye-opener. Talk about meeting the dregs of humanity. It was like being in another world. They sent me to an FE college in Soho, believe it or not. To teach maths...What a place. Bored apprentices on day release, arrogant blacks slouching around - Jesus, they made me mad. I stuck it till Christmas, then moved back in with my mother.'

He paused to stub out his cigarette and Will stood up.

'Shall we have a look round?' he said. 'We haven't got very far.'

'Aye, okay,' said Barry. 'I suppose that's why we're here after all.'

He heaved himself up from the bench and they walked past the changing huts and down the little hill. Barry got back into his stride.

'Anyway, luckily I landed a job as a research analyst with a West Midlands company. I say "luckily" because at least I was in the right profession, but otherwise - well, you know the demographics of that area. I began to understand why they call it the Black Country. West Indians, Asians, Muslims - we had the lot.'

'I think the name has more to do with the coal seams,' said Will. 'And the air pollution, the soot from heavy industry. It turned the white workers black.'

'I dare say, but I'm talking about the real thing - not the bloody Black and White Minstrels. Anyway I stuck that out for three years, then managed to get a job up here with ICI which was better all round.'

They were walking towards the woodland border now. A pair of fenced-in tennis courts stood empty over to their left.

'I was looking for the dyke when you arrived,' said Will. 'D'you remember the dyke?'

'The dyke? What was that?'

'The little stream where we used to catch tadpoles.'

'Oh, that. Well it was never very much in the first place, was it?'

Will slowed down and then stopped. This was near enough. Faint sunlight in the sky and a smattering of daisies at their feet. A fifty yard walk in a straight line out between the silver birches and back onto the street.

'I'll tell you what I do remember,' said Barry looking about. 'I remember having one of our smelly shoe fights round here. Remember? You tried to keep your pump pressed over the other person's nose.'

Will remembered the smell of dirt and sweat engrained in leather.

'I remember because that old biddy who used to be your piano teacher walked past and told us off. Or said something...'

'Miss Mellor? She was a sweet lady...'

'She had a nervous breakdown in the end, didn't she? All because of your piano playing.'

Will had told that joke himself so many times and so much better.

'She was burbling on about not throwing stones at the birds and she kept looking at me. I suspect she thought I was a bad influence.'

'She probably thought that's what boys do.'

13

'It's odd though, isn't it?' said Barry. 'Why we remember some things and not others. There must be thousands of events in your past that have gone from your mind for ever.'

'The past is another country,' ventured Will.

'I've heard that saying before.' Barry paused to mull it over. 'It's the present that's another country though. Certainly not the one we grew up in...'

'Well, things change...'

'Things change, obviously. And round here it hasn't been too bad. But when you look at the country as a whole, things have gone haywire. We're ruled from Brussels, we're dependent on Asian countries for cheap goods and we've been invaded. Our so-called Commonwealth cousins have been allowed to sail in by the boatload and breed as much as they like. Aided and abetted, of course, by the do-gooders, the social workers, the lefties...'

Will braced himself to speak.

'Anyway, why are we standing here?' said Barry. He consulted his watch. 'It's five to twelve. If we go that way' - he indicated over his shoulder - 'we can see the rest of the park and get to the Ship for some food.'

'I'm sorry Barry, but I have to go...'

It was rather abrupt, he knew. And Barry looked confused.

'But I thought we agreed to go for lunch?'

Will sighed.

'Barry...let me put it this way. I don't really think we have much in common any more - you know? So if it's all the same to you, I'd rather not.'

A new light dawned in Barry's eyes.

'Don't tell me you believe in all that stuff about "multiculturalism"? I should have guessed.' He shook his head. 'You've been away too long.'

'I've stayed away, Barry. I live elsewhere now. And I don't worry about "the blacks".'

'Well I suppose people have to put up with them in London and the big towns. For the time being, at least. But we don't want them *here*. We don't really want them anywhere - full stop. And most of them don't *want* to be here. They spit on our pavements as if they're spitting on us. They came here because their own pox-ridden countries are so poor.'

Will surprised himself by how calm and matter-of-fact he felt in the face of this outburst.

'Barry, they're human beings just like us. We grew up with people who spit on the pavement. Have you forgotten? A nice white boy spat in my face once.'

'They don't belong in *our country*. That's the point. They have homes where they came from. Look at our history - we're a white island race.'

'But why are you so obsessed with this? I haven't seen a black face in this town since I've been here.'

'It's only a matter of time, Will.'

'Barry, you're an intelligent guy. You were brighter than me at school. Why are you so bothered by race? By difference in skin colour? By *difference*? It's a fact of life.'

'Of course, there's *difference* but never the twain shall meet. That's what I believe. It threatens to turn us into a nation of mongrels.'

'Jesus Christ!'

'And the way I feel is the way most people feel around here if you take the trouble to ask. And not just around here either.' He hesitated and looked at his watch. 'Look, why don't we go for that drink? A couple of pints, a bite to eat and you never know. We might see a bit more eye to eye.'

For a moment, Will was tempted. He saw the two of them sitting in the pub, food and drink on the table, a shaft of sunlight sloping through the window, music in the background, alcohol loosening their minds... He shook his head.

'I don't think so, Barry. So long...' And that was all he said. There was no point in wasting any more words. He began the trek towards the silver birches.

'You'll realise what I'm talking about one day,' Barry called after him. It felt as if he was back in childhood after one of those silly squabbles which end with someone walking off. *I'm not playing any more*. And what was Barry shouting now? 'The one about the African wedding.' Unbelievable. 'Why do they spread dung down the sides of the aisle?' He'd heard it before except it had been a Jewish wedding then.

He passed between the birches and crossed the road. Around the corner was his childhood street more or less unchanged except for all the new front doors and white window frames and dazzling white sills. He imagined some evangelical salesman going from doorstep to doorstep spreading the gospel of home improvement. And here was his childhood house...yet how small and ordinary and characterless it appeared in spite of its makeover. There were no net curtains but the interior was a dark void. He remembered the coloured glass panels in the old front door and the solid wooden gate that had hung between the brick posts. Our castle, his father used to call it.

As he went on, another memory came back to him. How as a young boy he would run to the end of this street out of impatience or just for the joy of it. How his legs would work like pistons and the houses flash by and the main road come forward to meet him. Now the paving slabs stretched ahead and he could only go one step at a time and endure the tedium. Towards the end of the street, he passed a house with a poster in the window showing an arc of sunlight glowing over a mountain range and the message 'Be Patient and Understanding'.

Oh, I will, thought Will, smiling. I *will*. I'll stay for another day or two, but after that - let me go. Let me say goodbye to my folks, walk to the station, holdall in hand and board the train at Platform No 1. Then take me away, InterCity 125 diesel locomotive with your mighty power car. Take me back where I belong, over the hills and far away. Take me back home.

In My Beginning

Everything was strange for the first few seconds after she awoke that morning. The things she could see - the ceiling, the light fittings, the top panes of the windows - were unfamiliar. The voices she could hear were not ones she knew. She didn't actually ask herself: *where am I?* The question echoed all by itself in her head.

Of course, it didn't take long to remember. She was in hospital. Bill had brought her in yesterday. He was back at home now. She had never had an operation before but she mustn't be frightened. It had to be done. And they would take care of her in this place.

There were only six beds in Ward G2 and only four of them were occupied. It was small compared to the ward next door where they had booked her in, but she was glad to be in here. It was calmer. She heard the rattle of a trolley going past in the corridor outside. Then footsteps on the parquet floor and the creak of a starched apron as one of the nurses came over from the desk.

'Good morning, Irene. How are you feeling?'

'Oh, not so bad, thank you.'

She cleared her throat.

'Did you sleep all right?'

'It took me a little while to get off, but then I slept.'

In fact, it had taken her a long while and the night nurse must have thought she was asleep because she had gone out into the corridor to talk to someone else, another nurse. And then they had come into the ward and carried on talking and Irene didn't like to turn over because then they would know that she was still awake. She remembered hearing the bell of a fire engine and the hour striking from a nearby clock but she couldn't count all the chimes because of the two nurses talking. But it went on for so long that it must have been midnight. And then there had been loud voices in the big ward and someone running along the corridor and the second nurse had gone and doors had banged...But she must have fallen asleep soon after that.

'That's normal, dear, on your first night. You'll soon get used to everything. Are you ready to sit up now?'

The nurse sorted out her pillows, then turned to the next bed. Irene blinked at the ward clock. It said ten past seven. Bill would already be up and about. He would have gone to the bathroom first and that always took a while because of his piles. Then he would have to make breakfast for himself. They had already eaten their weekly ration of bacon and eggs - he had insisted on that because *you don't know what the food's going to be like in hospital* - so he would have to make porridge and she had shown him the best way to do that on Sunday. Then he would probably have a slice of toast with jam and two cups of tea from the pot! She smiled at the thought of him sitting alone at the dining table listening to the 8 o'clock news.

'Good morning, Irene! Nice to see you're still smiling!'

This came from Vera who was sitting up in the bed opposite. She was bright and brassy and Irene wasn't sure yet whether she was going to like her. But she said good morning. The lady next to her was also propped up on pillows, but she looked rather pale and frail. Nevertheless she managed a weak smile and a wave.

'I was thinking of my Bill at home. Sitting on his own, eating his breakfast and drinking his two cups of tea.'

'Oh, bless him! I'm sure he'll be all right, love,' said Vera. 'They can cope without us for a few days, you know. After all, they won the war for us, didn't they?'

Irene nodded. She didn't say that Bill had been a fireman in their town and hadn't really seen much of the war. He'd been classified as 'fit for home service only' due to poor eyesight and other medical problems but that had happened before they'd met and he'd never really talked about it. He was Leading Fireman Faraday back then and she'd been taken on as a switchboard girl at the station. He was three years older, a real gentleman and a good-looker too in her opinion. She'd had suitors before but they'd come and gone. Some of them had only wanted one thing. Then the war had started and a lot of men had gone overseas. *Be patient, Irene*, her mother had said to her. *There's someone for everyone out there.* And after a few days of courtship from Bill, she knew she'd met that someone. They'd married just before her twenty ninth birthday. Some of Bill's colleagues had formed a guard of honour outside the church, holding their axes in the air. They didn't see them so much now but it had been a wonderful day.

'They can do an awful lot can men, you know,' said Marjorie from the bed on her right. 'If they have to. Of domestic things, I mean...It's just that they prefer to leave most of it to us.'

'Well, the home is the woman's domain, really, isn't it?' said Vera.

Irene felt sad at those words. Home was Bill's domain just as much as hers. He wasn't one of those who go out at night to the pub or club leaving their wives alone. He was a good, honest man and the breadwinner whose salary helped to pay for their little house and garden. They were happy in each other's company. *Only one thing would make us happier*, thought Irene, *and that's why I'm here*. She swung her legs out of the bed and reached for her slippers.

'I just need to go to the toilet,' she said to the nurse

'Of course, Irene. Can you remember how to get there, dear?'

'Ay, I think so.'

'Just ask one of the ladies in G1 if you're not sure.'

She put on her dressing gown and padded across to the door.

'We'll send a search party for you Irene if you don't come back,' called Vera.

She walked down the short corridor, through the double doors and into the big ward. There was more of a 'buzz' in this ward although nothing much seemed to be happening other than nurses going to and fro checking on patients. She counted ten beds on each side as she walked along and returned the 'good mornings' from some of the women and the smiles and fluttery waves from others. Halfway down, she passed the bed of a lady who had also been admitted yesterday - a pale white-haired figure lying still between the sheets though her eyes watched Irene. Seventy years old and here for an operation, so they had heard!

At the end of the ward, she emerged into a long corridor which smelt strongly of polish. A man in a porter's jacket walked past her and two nurses talking as they hurried along, but no other patients seemed to be about. Irene felt rather vulnerable wandering around in her dressing gown and slippers. It felt a bit like being in a dream. She passed the entrance to another ward and then, on the left, she recognised the short corridor that branched off with a big notice board and two lifts and then the male and female toilets. To her relief, no-one was inside and she slipped quickly into one of the cubicles.

Her spirits improved on the way back. A very cheerful man who was pounding along the corridor, arms swinging, said 'good morning, madam' to her in the posh voice of a doctor or consultant. He made her smile. And in the big ward, the breakfast trolley had arrived and one of the nurses was helping to give out bowls of porridge. She found the familiar smell comforting.

'Breakfast's on the way, ladies!' she said as she re-entered G2.

'About time. I'm starving,' said Vera.

Soon the ward door opened again and the catering lady pulled her trolley in. She looked a long-suffering type, thought Irene, and her 'Good Morning' was rather weary. But the porridge when brought round was still hot enough and she got a little dollop of raspberry jam in it to improve the taste. That was followed by two slices of toast - cold, inevitably - but thinly spread with more jam and finally a white mug of tea with two sugars.

'Just what the doctor ordered,' she said.

The nurse smiled as she took the porridge bowl and plate away.

'Doctor Addis will be coming round later this morning, so you'll find out what else he's going to order.'

She came back from the trolley and stood beside Irene.

'You're not worried are you dear?'

Irene nodded.

'I am a little bit,' she said. 'I've never had an operation before. I've never been in hospital even.'

The nurse put her hand on Irene's shoulder and squeezed gently.

'It's only a minor operation that you're having. There's no need to worry about it. Lots of women go through it and you'll be much better afterwards.'

A little later, the nurse brought them each a bowl of hot soapy water so that they could wash their hands and faces and apply some make-up if they wanted to.

'Ooh, blimey - another fire engine,' said Irene as she was powdering her face. 'That must be the third or fourth I've heard this morning.'

'Oh, that's London Road,' said the nurse. 'Just up the road near the train station. It's the main fire station round here - that's why it's so busy.'

The name had a familiar ring. Where? - of course, from the war. What was she thinking of, forgetting so quickly? Bill had done some training there just before they'd met. He'd told her about it on one of their first dates.

'It was very important during the war,' said the nurse. 'The king and queen visited it once. And there was a big air raid shelter down in the basement.'

'Yes I know,' said Irene. 'I was in the Fire Brigade. That's where I met my husband. We knew about London Road.'

'What would we have done without the fire brigade, dear?' said Marjorie. 'They did a wonderful job. It must have been terrifying at times.'

'Oh aye, they were no army dodgers,' said Vera. 'People used to look down on them, didn't they? Until the bombs started falling...'

Irene felt a tear trickling down her cheek and told herself to stop it. Take a deep breath and stop it. Her hand went to the powder puff again. She didn't think of Bill as a hero - just someone who had done his duty in the best way he could. 'Steadfast' - that was the word one of his pals had used to describe him.

'And the women too,' said Vera. 'What did you do in the fire service, Irene?'

'Oh, I was just a telephonist. On the station exchange...'

'That's a vital job,' said the lady next to Vera whose name she remembered was Joan. 'My cousin became a motorcycle dispatch rider. She was only twenty three at the time. She'd never driven anything in her life before.'

'I used to go out with the mobile canteen,' said Vera. 'I never learnt to drive it though - that was another girl. I just made the bloomin' tea.'

While the conversation went on, Irene reached into the drawer of her bedside table and took out the new notepad that she'd bought and one of the nice sharp pencils that Bill had given her. He was a clerk now and brought them home from work. She thought of him sitting in the armchair doing the crossword and putting the pencil behind his ear when he'd finished. She found the hospital address on her admission letter, then wrote it down carefully in the top right corner of the first page. The paper was thin and unlined but it would do. After only a second's thought, she began writing.

Tuesday evening

Dear Bill,

Well Bill I have settled down at last. The Girls here are very friendly, we know everybody History about one another now., what are names are, and were we come from and all the rest. The Sister is very nice and polite to you and the 2 nurses of our ward is to. There are 20 women in the other ward, I do not know what they are in for, but I have to go through that ward if you want to go to the WC. and it is a long walk to get there and you know what I am like. Bill I have just been told the Doctor is coming, so I will finish this later.

I am here again, the Doctor has just been, and has asked me all particulars. he says there is nothing wrong with me only, what I am in for and that is why he is going to examin me to night for. The Doctor says it is only a little operation I require & I should be having it this week. Everybody tells me not to worry about it & I will feel better after. I hope you can read this letter, Bill for I am trying to do my best. So don't worry about me, I am not worrying, only about you hoping you get on alright, do not forget to read yourself to sleep at night. I will write to you again tomorrow to keep you going in letters so you will not get lonely.

Well this is all I have to say to you for the presant "cheer up" I will be home soon.

Best love from your wife Irene

She added thirty five kisses in five slanting rows up to the edge of the paper.

That evening, true to his word, Doctor Addis came back to examine her. One of the nurses drew the curtains around her bed, then pulled her blankets back. Without being asked, Irene pulled down her knickers and lifted her nightdress. She knew she had to get it over with.

'Don't worry, Mrs Faraday. This won't take long. Just relax.'

His hand was cold as he placed it on her abdomen and she gasped a little. He pressed down in various places. She thought how he was the only man apart from Bill to have touched her down there.

'Now if you could just bend your knees please, we're going to put your legs in these stirrups for support.'

Irene did as she was told and soon her legs were hoisted in front of her. This was the point where she stared hard at the ceiling.

'This might cause a little discomfort but it won't take long.'

He inserted that thing, whatever they called it, and started to probe. It *was* uncomfortable and she didn't know whether it was going to get worse. She lay still, gripping her tummy muscles. The nurse patted her shoulder. Doctor Wright back home had explained what they would do and she had talked to Bill about it the night before last. *Just lie back and think of England* he'd said. *Like you do with me.* And she had giggled. Well she didn't have much choice but to lie back, did she? And despite everything, she wanted to smile at the memory of Bill's words, but that wouldn't do. Ah! That was...she felt on the verge of tears. What was the matter with her? It wasn't that bad. She heard the nurse whispering *try and relax and breathe normally, Irene.* Yes she must do that. Breathe in, breathe out. She could hear Vera and Jean talking. Breathe in, breathe out. There went the bell of another fire engine. Breathe in...she felt the thing being removed.

'There we are, Mrs Faraday,' said Doctor Addis. 'All over.'

He went to have a word with Sister. The nurse waited while Irene pulled her knickers back up, then covered her with the blankets again.

'I expect you'd like a cup of tea now, wouldn't you?'

'Ooh, yes.'

The nurse bent forward beside her.

'And a biscuit?'

'Ooh, yes please.'

'Okay. I'll go and get some for you, then we'll sit you back up again. Just have a little rest.'

When Doctor Addis came back, he was smiling.

'Everything's fine, Mrs Faraday. I've had a word with Sister and we'll operate on Friday morning. As I've said before, it's only a minor op and there's absolutely nothing to worry about.'

'Ok, doctor. Thank you.'

He wrote something on a clipboard, then looked down at her.

'It's a family you want, isn't it?'

'I hope so, doctor. I hope so.'

He nodded and smiled, then slipped through the curtains and departed.

Eventually, the nurse brought her the cup of tea and two biscuits, then drew the curtains back.

'Dah dah,' said Vera. 'All done?'

'All done. And I'm going to have the operation on Friday.'

'Oh, you'll be out of here in no time, love.'

On Friday morning, they got her ready. *What a performance*, she wrote later to Bill. With the nurse's help, she put on a short coat, tied a piece of cloth like a large handkerchief round her head and pulled on a thick pair of socks like the ones that fishermen wear. It was *not very ladylike*. Then she sat on the chair by the bed and waited for the trolley. She felt nervous but Marjorie had done the same yesterday for her operation and was now quite cheerful, so perhaps it wouldn't be too bad.

The trolley came, she lay on it and the porter wheeled her through brown and cream corridors, down in a rattling lift, along another corridor and into the theatre. What a funny name for it, she thought. She and Bill had gone to the theatre a lot when they were courting during the war. The Palace Theatre and the Grand…She was lifted on to the operating table. There were lights overhead and people wearing face masks and that smell like cleaning fluid. Then somebody spoke close to her head. *Are you ready now, Mrs Faraday…just relax and take deep breaths.* And the black rubber mask came down over her face and she did as she was told and soon the darkness engulfed her.

When she began to come round, she was still half-dreaming about all the troops stationed around her town during the latter stages of the war. The soldiers and sailors, the Polish airmen, the Canadians and the American GIs. She mustn't mention it because Bill might feel jealous. His sister had married a GI and gone off to live in America! Not that she'd ever thought of that, but some of them were smashing fellows. What good times they'd had going to the pictures and dancing. Without ever getting tipsy either. Sometimes, if it wasn't for the blackout...

'How are you feeling now, Irene?' asked the nurse.

Saturday

My dear Bill,

How are you feeling this morning, I am feeling fine except, I have just had a few words with the doctor about my operation, and he says for my own good I have to have this thing in 7 days and I will be quite all right after. So I will be in here longer than we thought Bill, but I would rather do that than have to come back in here again with it wrong. I only hope I do not have to come any more for some of the women here have some awfull complaints, mine is only small to theres.

Vera left this morning and kissed us all goodbye before she left, it will be quite without her. It is pouring with rain here as well. When you come on Wednesday Bill, do not forget my curlers, a clean hand towel and my talcum powder and the News of the World. The Fire Engines from this Fire Station round here, keeps turning out all day long. It is London Road were you did your training before we met.

Anyway do not worry about me, I will be fine here. I could not get any better treatment If I was Princess Elizabeth and that's true, for they will not see anybody in pain. I am just going to use the bed pan, I will take one of these home for a souvenier, to put in your bookcase, what do you say.

Well Bill, Cheerio, Keep Smiling Till I Come Home To You, I Love You, Your Irene.

She had very little room left for five rows of kisses, but managed somehow to squeeze them in.

The days went by. They heard that the old lady in G1 had her operation and was *in a stable condition*. They asked Sister if she would be all right, but Sister was rather prim about it and would say only that *Miss Timms is as well as can be expected*. Next day the sky went very dark and there was a thunder storm. The day after, it was lovely and the sun *shone on me and my bed, the first time since I have been here, so it is a good sign* she wrote to Bill. Marjorie went home with a wave and a smile and was replaced by Cynthia. Joan left after promising to look her up one day and she was replaced by Martha. Vera's bed was empty for quite a few days and then along came a chirpy young woman called Ida who lived in the same town as Irene. They went through all their life histories again and Irene thought how lucky she was to have such good companions. And they all helped each other out as well. It was such a sociable ward that the nurses from the big ward used to drop by some evenings for a rest and a chat. On Wednesday evening they had a sing song. She needed her spirits lifting because that was the day Bill visited. He looked so smart and brought everything she'd asked for and even some flowers from their garden at home. He'd got there early, he told her, before visiting hours.

'I walked along the canal, up and down that main road out there, into the News Theatre across the street, all the time carrying these blooming flowers.'

He told her all his news. How the air raid shelter on their road had finally been pulled down. How he'd got on with his cooking and housework. How her friend Amy had called to see her, not knowing she was in hospital. How her brothers and sisters sent their love. Despite his shyness, he talked to all the other ladies and when he smiled his eyes shone with all the attention. She cried a little after he'd gone, then pulled herself together. It wouldn't be long now. Ida and the other girls all said how lucky she was to have a man like that.

And sure enough a few days later the doctor examined her and gave her the good news.

Saturday

My Dear Husband,

Top of the morning to you, it is a lovely day here and I am feeling fine. The time is 7.45 and we have just had breakfast. Well Bill I had my final examination last night by the Doctor and he has passed me fit to come home on Tues. and what an exam. I will tell you about it when I get home. I have not got that thing in now, when they, the nurses came to make our beds, this morning I jumped over to the other side of the bed, and there eyes popped out, they did not know, I had not got my (GI) in.

26

Every night before I go to sleep and when I wake up the first and last thing I do is to think of you Bill and what you will be doing. I know you will have missed me a lot, but it will be far better, now this job has been done, and over with and no more worries. On Monday Bill, will you get a couple of loaves in and if you can get some pork saus. from the Coop, that's all I want.

We are going to have another Sing Song in our ward on Monday night, there are 3 of us leaving on Tuesday they will be glad to get rid of us. Ridgeway Ave will seem strange to me, but I am looking forward to coming home, we will celebrate. See you my dear on Tuesday morning and tell them off at work, if they don't like you taking another day off.

Best love Irene, T.T.F.N Irene

It wasn't until she had sealed the envelope and pressed into place the coloured stamp of George VI with her thumb over his neatly parted hair that Irene realised she hadn't added any kisses. She turned the envelope round and drew a big kiss across the bottom of the flap. She hoped Bill would notice.

They had their sing song on Monday evening. It went so well that G1 and the next ward further down the corridor kept sending their nurses to ask for different songs. And so they belted out I've Got a Lovely Bunch of Coconuts, Cruising Down the River, Bye Bye Blackbird, Knees Up Mother Brown, Roll Out the Barrel, On the Sunny Side of the Street and many many more until Sister thanked them very much and told them they just had to rest. The nurse gave each of them a cup of Ovaltine last thing before lights out, but it took Irene quite a while to get to sleep.

At 11 o'clock the next morning on a lovely sunny day, Bill arrived to take her home. They embraced and Irene gave him a big kiss though she wasn't sure if it was the right thing to do in front of the others and Bill looked a little embarrassed. They were the first to leave. Martha's husband was on the way and Cyn's sister was coming after lunch. Ida had to stay in a few more days but she and Irene exchanged addresses and said how they must meet up. She gave all the girls a kiss and received a kiss from the two day nurses. The Sister gave her a warm handshake and wished her well. Bill took her suitcase and held the ward door open.

27

As they walked through G1, some of the women waved and called good bye but rather quietly. Then they got to the old lady's bed. It was neatly made and empty. Startled and apprehensive, she stopped and asked the woman in the next bed.

'She passed away in her sleep, poor dear. They couldn't wake her this morning.'

'Oh no...after going through that operation and all!'

'They think it might have been the strain of that...Didn't your nurses tell you?'

'Perhaps they didn't want to spoil our last morning. We knew she was on the danger list. Didn't she hear our sing-song last night?'

'If I'm honest I don't think she was aware, love. But I think the nurses were grateful because it took everyone's mind off it.'

Irene said goodbye and left the ward a little more subdued than she had entered it. As they waited for the lift, she told Bill.

'We were all keeping our fingers crossed for her. Fancy being operated on at that age - 70 years old.'

'Aye, it wouldn't have happened a few years ago. Look at my dad - gone at 63.'

'I suppose so.'

There were other people in the lift, so they didn't talk about it. But Irene saw the old lady lying there again, still and white as a ghost.

When they were outside on the pavement, Bill put the suitcase down and they hugged and kissed again.

'I've missed you.'

'I've missed you, Bill! I'm glad it's all over.'

'It's all for the best. We can give it another go now. Well, when you're ready...'

She laid her head against his chest.

'Listen, shall we walk a bit, old girl, and get the bus near Piccadilly?'

She nodded.

'I ought to start using my legs again.'

'Come on, then.' He picked up the suitcase. 'Shanks's pony.'

'Shanks's pony,' she repeated.

And so they linked arms and walked away through the red brick canyons of the city. It felt odd at first and quiet like a Sunday. Even the fire station on London Road was silent. But they caught a bus around the corner and as it drove off, Irene glanced through the window and saw a bomb site ablaze with dark pink flowers.

'Look at those,' she said. 'Aren't they pretty?'

'Aye,' said Bill. 'Fireweed, they call it.'

And he squeezed her hand.

Runaway

The boy sat in a field that lay just beyond the last outgrowth of town. He had been stroking the edge of a blade of grass with the tender flesh of his middle finger, but now he pulled it from the earth and tried to bind it round his fist instead. When he looked up, he could see house gables and rooftops not far away, but the rest of the town spread out of sight to the west where the sun had begun its slow descent over the sea.

He had no watch but it was early in the evening, perhaps six o'clock or thereabouts. His parents would soon be expecting him home for tea, but he would not be there. Tonight, he would sleep near here, perhaps in one of the farm sheds that he had seen in the distance. Tomorrow, he would set off across the fields to the mysterious countryside beyond.

Throwing aside the blade of grass, he stretched out full-length on the ground, head resting on his duffel bag and gazed at the blue sky above. A small white butterfly flitted over him, then was gone. A car with a high-pitched engine whined along the road beside the field. He closed his eyes and listened to the sound as it fell slightly at a bend, soared upwards again, then gradually grew fainter. Now everything was still and peaceful again as if the whole world was at rest. This is what life would be like from now on. He would walk along the hidden lanes, track through woods like one of the native scouts in his book *Famous Indian Tribes* and climb hillsides to check the lay of the land. He would stop whenever he liked. At night, he would sleep in barns or under hedges. And somewhere along the way he would meet people who would become his friends. Fellow wanderers, gypsies, fairground folk...

He opened his eyes and sat up quickly, alarmed that someone might be creeping up on him, but he was still alone. None of the gangs he was aware of would come this far in any case, but he knew it was dangerous to relax for too long. Two boys had done that in the park last summer, snaked on their bellies through the long grass towards him as he lay cloud-watching. Quite by chance he had jumped up and spotted them before it was too late...

Where was Roy? He opened the navy blue duffel bag and

rummaged around checking its contents. He had packed it quickly after coming home from school, knowing his parents would be back from work in an hour or so. He had also packed it sparsely, not wanting his departure to be obvious straight away. There was a rolled up nylon raincoat with hood, a pullover, a shirt, a T-shirt, one pair of underpants, one pair of socks, a handkerchief, the compass that he'd used in the Cubs, a pen and the diary that had been a Christmas present. A glass in the bathroom still had some old toothbrushes in it and he had taken one of those. He had pulled some toilet paper off the roll and had also taken a few tissues from a box in the lounge. Finally, he had squeezed in a small bottle of lemonade and two chocolate bars bought on the way home from school. His penknife was in his trouser pocket, along with a few coins that remained from his weekly allowance. He was ready. He took out the diary which had only a few entries in it from early January and wrote against the date: 'Left home at 4.55'. Then he put this back in the duffel bag, moving the chocolate bars aside as he did so. If Roy didn't appear soon, he would have to eat at least one of those.

A few minutes later, he heard the call - a sound that could have been either a muted war cry or an owl hooting. Then Roy emerged from a gap in the hedge on the eastern border of the field. Will lifted his right arm in salute and watched his friend walk steadily closer, bouncing a football and stepping smartly around clumps of grass.

'I was expecting you to come that way,' he said when Roy drew near and nodded towards the stile off the main road and,not far beyond it, the cul-de-sac of new houses where Roy's family lived.

'Nah, I wanted to throw them off the trail.'

'Who's *them*?'

'Oh, just family, neighbours, anyone who might know me. Told them I was going to play football for half an hour. There's a field on the other side of the road where we sometimes do that. So I walked up to that, then crossed the road out of sight because it bends round, then came through" - he paused, gazing upward while counting on his fingers - "three hedges, across two fields, down a ditch, past the pond, down a ditch again and then into this field.'

He concluded this matter-of-fact recital by pulling a small paper bag from inside his shirt and setting it down on the ground.

'That's the best I could do, Willie boy. Didn't want to make it too obvious.'

Will opened the bag. Inside was a pork pie, a triangle of cheese spread and a packet of crisps.

Wow - that's terrific.' He felt happy and reassured, not only by the food but by the fact that Roy was taking this seriously. He took a bite out of the pie and watched as Roy sat down, crossed his legs and glanced around the field. He was shorter than Will, slim and agile with glossy black hair, olive skin and rich brown eyes. He looked at Will now and flashed a facetious "here I am" smile.

'Nice evening, isn't it?'

Will nodded.

'How long have you lived round here?'

'How long?' Roy shrugged. 'Few years...my mum and dad used to live in a small village, so they wanted to be near the countryside. I've got to know all this area quite well.' And he gestured around at the fields and hedges and distant copses. 'My dad says we're an outdoors family. We go camping every year and climb mountains and sail on boats and stuff. Last year, we had a canal boat for a week.'

'Wow,' said Will through a mouthful of pie. Even though they were classmates, he didn't really know Roy that well outside school. He had only talked to him about his plan at lunch break because he knew somehow that Roy lived near by. Now he began to feel envious.

'It actually got a bit boring after a while, though. We had to keep stopping at locks and so on - you know, where you have to wind the lock gates open.'

Will didn't know, but nodded as he unwrapped the silver foil around the cheese.

'And my sister actually fell in. She fell in the water!' Roy hooted. 'She's only eight and not a good swimmer so my dad had to jump in after her. He was cross.'

'We usually go to holiday camps,' Will said. 'Me and my mother, that is. My dad stays at home.'

Roy looked thoughtful.

'I wouldn't mind going to a holiday camp,' he said as if struck by this idea for the first time. 'What do you actually do there? My dad says it's a bit like the army, except they force you to have fun.' He giggled. 'You live in huts and they wake you in the morning through some loudspeaker system.'

Will shook his head.

'They don't do that where we've been. You have your own little chalet and you can get up when you like though you might miss breakfast. They have lots of games and competitions and shows, they have indoor and outdoor swimming pools, they have places where you can play table tennis and snooker, they have wrestling matches that you can go and watch - they're brilliant...and everything's free. Oh and they have a ballroom where they play rock'n'roll in the evening.'

'Hmm, sounds okay,' said Roy. 'In the evening when we go camping, my sister and I run around and play outside with other kids, then we have hot chocolate in the tent and play cards and have quizzes. Then we walk through the dark with a torch to the toilet block and brush our teeth before bed. And if you look up you can see all the stars. I could show you the Plough now if it was dark and Vega and probably the North Star too.'

Will was impressed though he tried not to show it. His father read books on space travel and other worlds, but had never told him much about this world and the night sky. He offered Roy a crisp and tried to think of something to say.

'I like looking at the moon...' was all he could manage

'So why are you running away from home, then?'

He shrugged. It was difficult to put it in words.

'I'm just...fed up. My parents are too strict. They make me do things I don't want to like piano lessons and going to Sunday School. My dad gets really cross sometimes; my mum - well, she hasn't smacked me for a while but she used to. Once' - he hesitated - 'she hit me with a poker.'

'A poker! What - hard?'

'No, not hard. She rapped my hand with it...but it wasn't very nice. Have you ever been treated like that?'

Roy shook his head silently.

'I suppose...she once told me that her father hit her with a strap when she was naughty, so...Anyway, it's not just that. I want to have a more exciting life. We never do anything like you do with your parents. I want to have adventures...'

He dug his hand into his duffel bag and drew out the two chocolate bars.

'Want one of these?'

Roy shook his head and they sat in silence for a few moments. Will glanced westward. The sun was getting close to the horizon and the sky was a broad band of rosy red. Suddenly, Roy did a backward somersault, then a forward somersault, then tossed his black fringe back and grinned.

'Shepherd's delight,' he said. 'It should be a fine night. You like looking at the moon, so what could you see last night?'

'I dunno. I don't look at it every night - only when I see it.'

'Well, you wouldn't have seen anything - it's a new moon. That means no moonlight. *Scary*... but - you'll be able to see the stars. And you might actually sleep better if there's no moonlight.'

'Uh huh.'

'So you're going to sleep somewhere round here?'

'Yep. Just to get used to it.'

'In a barn?"

'Yep".

'Okay." Roy did another backward somersault, then sprang to his feet. 'Come on then. Let's go and have a look before it gets dark...'

Will stood and took a swig from his lemonade bottle while Roy bounced his ball. Then he slung his duffel bag over his shoulder and the two boys walked together to the edge of the field. They went through the gap in the hedge and stopped while Roy looked around.

'There is a right of way over these fields, but it's best to keep a look out for the farmer and his men. Tell you what...' - he spun the football round in the air - 'I'll just hide this somewhere, pick it up later.'

He side-footed the ball carefully into the scrub, then they set off alongside the hedge, although after about ten yards Roy abruptly veered out into the middle of the field.

'I'd normally keep to the hedges but there's something I want to show you.'

They came to a belt of tall grass, slender plants and reeds and then Will realised they were standing over a pond, a stretch of dark water that lay absolutely still before them. Following Roy, he scrambled down the low bank and stood on a patch of bare clay right at the water's edge.

'My dad's caught carp in here,' Roy said. 'It's deeper than you might think. I haven't got a proper rod yet, but he's let me reel them in a couple of times. Last year, though, I caught one just with a piece of string.'

'Wow.'

'You need to have a worm, of course - a nice juicy worm - and find a thorn, a long thorn, the longer the better. You make a hole in the worm with your pen knife, yes?'

'Yes...'

'Then you run the thread through the worm and attach it to the thorn so they're close together. The thorn is your hook.'

'Uh-huh...'

'When the fish takes the worm, the thorn gets stuck in its mouth. It panics and starts to pull on the string. When you feel that, you pull the string out and hey presto - you've caught a fish.'

'Wow!' he said. Poor fish, he thought, seeing the thorn stuck in its mouth, the shock lodged in its eyes.

'The only trouble is' - Roy counted on his fingers - 'One, you might have to wait a long time. Two, you have to keep a tight hold on the string, otherwise it will slip out of your hand when the fish pulls. And that means - the fish will die a *sloww horrrrible* death under water and you'll have lost your supper. Come on!'

And they scrambled back up the bank and carried on walking. Near the corner of the field was a metal gate, stuck part-open in dry mud. They passed through the gap, turned left down a hollow and up again, then stepped carefully over a sagging barbed-wire fence into another large field. Roy looked around, then they set off across the field eventually turning at a right angle to walk lengthways but close to the hedge. They had been moving south or south east and Will felt as if they were getting into the real countryside at last. Glancing over his shoulder, he noticed that the sun had gone and the red glow in the sky was thinning out. Suddenly, Roy stopped.

'Listen!'

They listened. A faint breeze was stirring the leaves in some nearby trees, but apart from that all was quiet. Then he heard it, the sound that Roy's ears had picked up earlier, some distance away but piercing - a sound that was half-scream, half-screech. He felt his heart speed up.

'What is it?'

'An owl. A barn owl. They don't go "*woooo*".' He grinned. 'That means you might have company tonight if you're sleeping in a barn, though he'll be out hunting a lot of the time. Listen! There it goes again...'

They moved on and as they came close to the end of the field, Roy slowed and did an exaggerated mime of creeping with finger to lips. They passed through another part-open gate, then climbed carefully up a little ridge lined with tangled trees and scrub. Crouching, they peered through the thickets and there was the farmyard ten yards away with a rusting plough frame half-submerged in weeds at its edge. He was surprised how suddenly they had come upon it.

And not only that but a man was marching across the farmyard, his boots crunching on gravel, towards the main gate on their left. A black and white collie which had been following stopped and watched with its ears cocked as the man reached the gate and began to pull it shut. Will was startled to see a row of black furry objects hanging from the top bar, swaying slightly as it swung forward. The man fastened the gate with some sort of metal hasp, then paused for a few moments looking around. The two boys ducked their heads, then heard the boots set off again and the man's low voice talking to the collie. When they looked again, the backs of man and dog were disappearing from sight and then they heard the solid thud of a door closing.

'What were those black things on the gate? Rats?'

'No, rats are usually brown. Those are dead moles that he's probably caught in traps. There'll be plenty of rats about though.'

'Ugh.'

'That's the side of the farmhouse across the yard - it faces south. That's the cow shed in front of us.' He nodded towards a large black corrugated shed about thirty yards away. 'That's a barn that has all sorts of equipment in it and piles of wood.' He pointed at a large rather ramshackle shed on their right. 'You could sleep in there but it's a bit close to the farmhouse. On the other side of that cowshed is a hay barn - that's your best bet.'

'Okay. How do you know all this?'

'We come here some weeks to buy eggs and I've been with my father when he picks up manure for the garden. We bring an old bath tub to take it back in the car. Actually, I often just walk over like we've done and creep about and see what's going on. It's fun.'

'Yeah.'

'So - to get to the hay barn, you'll have to walk around past that gate and along the next field. You'll be able to see the barn over the hedge when you reach it and then I'm pretty sure there's a gap you can squeeze through. But remember...' - he held his fingers up again - 'One: keep quiet and stay well away from the main farmyard. There's another dog here somewhere, a terrier. You don't want them to hear you or smell you. And two: the farmer starts work early in the morning. So you'll have to be up early too. If you wake and it's broad daylight, well...' He grinned. 'You've overslept.'

'Won't a cock crow and wake me?'

'Probably. Try not to poo in your pants...'

And laughing, he scrambled back down the little ridge into the field with Will following.

'Listen' - Roy became serious again - 'I've got to go home now, but if you want, I'll walk to the barn with you.'

'It's okay. I'll just stay here until it gets a bit darker and then I'll go and have a look.'

'If you don't like the barn, you could always just sleep under a hedge. Or I know what...you could just go back home for tonight, tell your parents you were out playing or something - then set off early in the morning. After all, it's the weekend. That would give you more time to find somewhere to sleep tomorrow night.'

Will shrugged.

'I'll think about it.'

'Okay.'

Then Roy held his hand out like grown-ups do and wished him good luck. Will felt his long fine-boned fingers as they shook. After that, there was nothing more to say. Roy slipped back through the gate, then turned to give him a quick wave and a grin before setting off back across the field. Will followed through the gate and watched. No longer sticking to the hedgerows, Roy was half-running, half-skipping to the far corner. At one point, he did a cartwheel. At another, he stopped to pick something up from the ground, then carried on until, without looking back, he vanished into the pond field. Will felt as if he had been forgotten already.

He walked forward a little way looking for a gap in the thick hedge. It was difficult but he found a hole that he could crawl through on hands and knees, pushing his duffel bag through first. He emerged with scratched hands and kneecaps onto what was the access road to the farm - a narrow lane with patches of grit embedded in the surface and deep tyre tracks. And there about twenty yards away was the gate with the black lifeless creatures hanging against it. Where would he find the rats, he wondered - the live running rats? He had never seen one in real life before. He sat down carefully on the bank between clumps of slender yellow flowers and took the last remaining chocolate bar out of his duffel bag.

As he munched his way through it, he scanned the hedge opposite looking for another gap and thought he could see one nearer the gate. It was now definitely starting to get dark. From somewhere, he heard a sheep bleat a couple of times. A bird was singing near the farmyard, sweetly but sadly, stopping every now and then as if listening for a response. This is the dusk, he thought, the twilight hour seen through living room windows before the curtains are drawn. He finished the chocolate bar, thrust the wrapper into his trouser pocket and stood up. Without looking at the gate, he walked down the lane and examined the gap in the hedge. It was much bigger than the other one and he could crouch down in it and peer through. There was the cow shed and the back of the wooden barn that Roy had mentioned, but between them was another gate leading in and out of the farmyard and he realised that this field was where the cows would graze in the daytime. They would be let into it next morning after milking. He would have to be away very early...

He wandered back to the yellow flowers and sat down again. For a few minutes, he stayed there with his chin resting on his hands, staring at the ground. Somewhere behind him, a tree branch creaked like an old door and he looked round in fear. He knew what was going to happen. An owl was glaring at him in the barn, rats were running across the floor, the farmer was coming with his gun, gun, gun...It was no good. The high hedges along the lane were blackening in the gloom. The game was up. He had known all along it would happen. Inside him was a barrier that he couldn't get beyond or even approach, like that barred gate at the end of the lane. He had felt it before. In any case, what would be the point of sleeping here when he was only a few hundred yards from the town? Less than an hour's walk from his home? Perhaps if he set off again tomorrow morning as Roy had said, got far away from the town, found somewhere better to spend the night in plenty of time before dark...He stood up, shouldered his duffel bag and started to walk towards the main road. It had been an adventure anyway.

When he emerged from the lane, he crossed to the paved side of the road and followed it around the bend. There was a path with a signpost to a riding school, then a few isolated bungalows and houses started to appear and then the close in which Roy lived. He walked quickly past but there was no-one and nothing to see except for the flicker of television light in one of the nearest windows. Further on came a row of shops, closed and dark within, while on the other side the hedgerow came to an abrupt end and a redbrick pub with car park appeared. And then the town began properly with a roundabout, streets under lamplight branching off to left and right, a garage forecourt, a few shadowy people walking the pavements and a double-decker bus which swayed past glowing with light towards the last stop on its route. He stayed on the main road for a mile or so as it ran deeper into town, then turned right on to the avenue that led past the doctor's surgery and towards the park. He knew the park well. He had played in it most of his life. And on the far side screened by trees stood his house.

He approached a junction where another street bisected the road in front of him and then had a shock. Suddenly, as if in some hazy dream, his father appeared cycling across it. In the lamp light, Will saw the greying hair, the familiar blunt-nosed profile, the old brown jacket and black trousers clamped around the shins, the big feet resting on the pedals. He was squeezing the brake to slow down and peering the other way at the short road which led on to the park, but at any moment he would look this way. Instinctively, Will leapt behind a telegraph pole that stood against a garden wall. He held himself stiffly at attention against it, hoping that he couldn't be seen. After a few seconds, he peered cautiously around the pole, then ran to the corner. There was his father, toiling away on the heavy old black bike, facing a steep hill ahead. What if he went to the police?

'Dad!' he shouted but his father didn't hear. He ran after him along the pavement.

'Dad!' This time he saw his father's shoulders stiffen and watched him brake and come to a halt against the kerb. He looked over his shoulder and Will saw only the anger in his eyes.

'Sorry, I went to see someone out at Steyning after school and forgot the time.'

'Your mother's been worried stiff about you. I was just about to go to the police.'

'Sorry - look I'll run back across the park and see her.'

His father started to turn the bike and without waiting, Will ran back and around the corner, then down the slope. A group of older boys were leaning against a wall across the road and one of them shouted something in a jeering sort of way. Will ignored it and reached the first path in a network of paths that would lead him across the dark fields and back to his street and house. He looked up for a moment as he ran. Roy had been right - there was no moon but loads and loads of tiny stars that gleamed in the black sky above. He would learn their names, their - what was the word? - constellations. He thought of the address written at the front of his little diary - the address that went on and on: England, the Earth, the Solar System, the Milky Way, the Universe... Where was heaven then? Mr Hargreaves hadn't answered that question at Sunday School and had given him a cold look afterwards. Was he becoming a *trouble maker*? He glanced back and saw his father's bright headlamp getting nearer. He ran on with one hand gripping the cord of his duffel bag. He was running in a race - no, training for a race. His father was the coach pedalling furiously behind. They would soon be approaching the finishing post...

But now his ribs were hurting. He was getting a stitch. He reached the end of the rough ground and stopped for a few seconds, then padded along the tarmac path. At the edge of the park, he stopped again and bent over to squeeze his sides. Holding his breath, he heard the clank of a chain much closer than he'd thought. Without looking back, he stepped onto the pavement and pushed himself on. The home straight they called it...only a short distance to go. But he was more or less walking now. What was the use? The narrow beam of his father's headlamp crept up alongside him. He watched as it danced on the roadway.

Ginger

His first two attempts had been disastrous, but somehow the third
hoop soared through the air at just the right angle and fell neatly
over the wooden peg.

'Whoa,' said the man behind the stall. 'Third time lucky, eh?' He
licked the tip of his finger, pulled open a plastic bag and sauntered
over to a tank that they could just make out in the shade behind him.

'There aren't many have done that today, you know,' he said half-
turning to them as he dipped the bag into the tank. When he pulled it
out, three quarters full with gently rocking water, a little goldfish
could be seen turning and twisting inside it.

'You might have the knack, you know,' said the man as he fastened
the top of the bag. 'Want to try again?'

They smiled and shook their heads. He was only teasing.

'There you are then, son,' said the man as he passed the bag across
the counter. 'Put him in a bowl of water as soon as you get home and
he'll be fine.'

They thanked him and walked away across the grass. His mother
glanced back over her shoulder, then leaned confidentially towards
him.

'Did you see the tattoo on his arm? A ship's anchor and a mermaid.
That's funny as he was giving you a fish...'

Will smiled but gripped the bag tightly in his hand. He felt as if he
had been given a big responsibility and he was not used to it. Apart
from an old tortoise which he had shuddered to pick up, he had
never before owned a pet. What if it started to act crazy or went all
still or just conked out before they got home?

'What's my dad going to say?'

'Oh I don't know, but you've won it now. We'll talk him round.'

He had one more ride on the Speedway Racers while his mother
held the bag, then they bought drinks and wandered around in the
sunshine for a while, watching men hurling balls at the coconut shy
and donkeys padding up and down their strip, before finally heading
towards the gate.

'What should we call it?' his mother asked as they walked down the
road to the bus stop.

'Alphonse,' he said. 'Egbert. Attila...'

She looked down at the fish that was swaying calmly now in its little bag.

'How about something nice and simple like Ginger.'

He liked that. Ginger - the name of one of the "outlaws" in the *William* books. Will and Ginger...

'But we don't know if it's a boy fish or a girl.'

'Well, then - Ginger's perfect. It's used for girls too. Ginger Rogers, the film star...'

So Ginger, he or she was. Back home, his mother filled a large glass bowl with water and placed it carefully with a doily underneath on top of the radiogram in the front bay window. But he still had to keep hold of the bag.

'I've never done this before,' his mother said. 'But something tells me we should just let that water warm up a bit before Ginger goes into it.'

After a few minutes, though, she undid the rubber band around the neck of the bag and let Will immerse it in the bowl until the little fish swam out. They stood and watched as it flapped its fins and slowly circumnavigated its new temporary home, staring at the curved glass walls through curved glassy eyes. His mother brought some bread crumbs and he sprinkled them on the water, then sat a few feet away on the piano stool. At first, the fish ignored the crumbs floating above its head, then rose to inspect them, then finally - to his relief - started to nibble. *Manna from heaven* - the phrase came back to him from Sunday School. All was going well.

When his father came home from work, they gathered again around the bowl and awaited his verdict. He seemed to be in a good mood.

'Well, it'll be all right I suppose. We used to have one when I was your age - me and my sister - but somehow the cat got it. She was more upset than me. My sister, that is - not the cat.' Will grinned. 'They need regular fresh water and cleaning out, you know - and you'll have to help with that.' Will nodded. 'We'll also have to get some proper food and a tank for it. We can't keep it in that.'

'No,' said his mother. 'There'll be no more jelly for tea until I get that bowl back.'

His father smiled and Will saw the reflection of their three faces for a moment before Ginger turned sharply and sent the water rippling.

That evening, he sat with his father in the side-garden near the kitchen window. It was a fine warm evening with only the gentlest of breezes. He listened to the shouts of children playing further down the street and watched a pair of sparrows jump from the black guttering to the fence, then flit daringly to the bird table a few feet away where his mother had left more crumbs.

'Dad,' he said. 'You know when we get our shelter...'

'If we get one,' said his father from behind the evening paper.

'Will we be able to take Ginger into it with us?'

'Possibly. They're designed to provide shelter for two weeks so he might not have stunk us out by then.'

'Hmm. Well that's something else to add to our list then.'

'It's become a long list, hasn't it? Food and drink, bed linen, toiletries, books, card games...'

'My football game...'

'A radio...'

'Diaries...'

'Paper and pens - and now the new family pet.' He lowered the paper. 'Anyway, what's the point of saving a goldfish when all the other animals on the planet will die?'

Will felt a tremor inside at this wider vision of destruction, but he rallied.

'Hmm, yes, but Ginger won't know that all the other animals have died.'

'He won't know that *he's* died if we leave him where he is. It'll all be over in a flash. Anyhow, I don't think it's going to happen now. Krushchev's had the wind taken out of his sails over Cuba.'

'Hmm. Also Ginger wouldn't need any exercise...whereas if we had a dog, it would go mad.'

'Don't be a crackpot, Will. We don't want World War Three breaking out just so you can furnish a fall out shelter. It's not like building a den to play in, you know.'

'I know,' said Will, but he sighed nevertheless.

The next day his mother bought a tin of fish food flakes from the local Co-op and Will had to sprinkle a second helping on the water after Ginger devoured the first. On Saturday, they went to the Pet Emporium in town and bought a small tank which came with a bag of little coloured pebbles, a pair of aquatic plants and a filter pump. On Sunday morning, his mother filled the tank with water from the kitchen tap, then huffed and puffed as she carried it into the living room.

'Will - help me! Get hold of that end or I'll damage the radiogram.'

They lowered the tank gently onto a plastic mat and Will had fun for a while spreading out the pebbles and trying to create an underwater jungle effect with the plants. Then they attached the pump and he crawled under the radiogram to plug it in. It hummed and vibrated and sent a stream of small bubbles flowing across the surface.

'We might have to turn that off when we're listening to the radio,' said his mother.

Now came the moment to relocate Ginger whose bowl had been moved to one side. His mother brought in an old plastic jug.

'This is the only way we're going to do it.'

After two or three attempts, Will caught Ginger in the jug and then quickly tipped water and fish into the tank.

'Not like that! You'll scare the life out of it.'

'I was worried he'd jump out.'

He bent down and peered through the glass. The fish swam in and out of the plant fronds, then turned sharply towards him and for a moment its black bulging eyes did seem to gleam with anger before it dived down to root amongst the pebbles.

'Come on. Let's clear up and then you need to do some piano practice.'

A few minutes later, the noise of the pump was overcome for a while as the chords of Tchaikovsky's Piano Concerto No 1 in B Flat Minor crashed around the living room.

They left it a fortnight before cleaning out the tank. It was the last day of the school holiday and felt like the end of summer to Will even though the sun continued to shine. The previous day, they had discussed how best to tackle the job.

'Pour the dirty water down the drain outside,' said his father. 'Put the fish back in the jelly bowl while you're doing it. But don't get me involved. This is your show.'

Then his mother hit on a better idea. They would run some water into the bath and give Ginger a bit more room to swim about in. In the morning therefore, he helped her carry the tank into the bathroom and let Ginger loose in the bath. He watched the little creature swim up and down a few times before stopping as if confused. It seemed smaller than ever in the long clear stretch of water.

'It's like it's in a lake in a valley,' he said. But his mother wasn't listening.

'I'm not sure how we're going to do this,' she said, wiping her brow. At that moment, Will felt glad that his father wasn't involved.

'Let's take the plants out first.' And they put the two plants in the wash basin. Then, holding it at the corners, they took the weight of the tank in their hands and tilted it over the toilet, slowly pouring out as much of the murky water as possible without losing any of the pebbles.

'That's its poo,' said Will with a nod at the floating brown strands which he had seen emerging from Ginger's underside.

'Oh well, this is the best place for it then.'

After that, he carried the almost empty tank to the big sink in the kitchen where his mother showed him the best way to rinse and clean it before filling it again with fresh water. Then they hauled it back to the radiogram and his mother took the plastic jug to scoop up Ginger from the bath. She held her other hand over the jug in case Ginger was tempted to jump out and Will saw the thin and thick gold bands that sat unscathed on her ring finger.

'Well, there we are. That wasn't too bad,' she announced, looking at his father who briefly lowered the Sunday Express.

'What a palaver. And all for one little fish.'

The next day, Will met up with his school friend Davey and did the twenty minute walk across town.

'Remember last year,' said Will 'when someone cycled past shouting about what they were going to do to us when we got there?'

'Yeah. We must have stood out a mile - all neatly dressed in our new uniform.'

'Actually, they didn't do it to me until the next day and it wasn't that bad.'

'What the initiation ceremony?'

'Yeah, it hardly hurt at all.'

'Actually, we're not doing it, so I've heard.'

'Really? But it's our turn.'

'Well, that's what Ferdie said at the end of last term. We're going to be the first year not to do it. It's the beginning of a new era.'

'Wow.'

'So what've you been up to then? I only saw you that one time when I was with Phil on the bus.'

'Been to Butlins for a week with my mum. Played a lot of football with the kids round my way.'

'What, little nippers?'

'No - kids I used to go to primary school with. Went down to the sands a few times. Went to Livingstone Park. Went to the circus and the aquarium. Oh and I won a goldfish at Carlton Gala.'

'Uh huh.'

Davey then recounted everything that he'd been doing which took a long time - so long that by the time he'd finished, they were turning into the cobbled alley that led to the school's rear entrance. As they got halfway along, a bicycle bell rang behind them and a mocking voice sang out.

'Make way, make way.'

They stood to one side and watched an older boy with black quiffed hair ride past, leaning back casually in the saddle with one hand resting loosely on cow horn handle bars. A battered old satchel was slung across his back featuring a crude picture of a guitar encircled by silver beamed notes. He had dismounted when they reached the bike sheds and was talking loudly to someone else. They had to walk around the bike which was painted purple with the legend *Johnny Crud* in orange lettering on the down tube.

'Huh,' said Davey when they were safely past. 'Old hat.'

'Yeah. Who does he think he is?'

'Johnny Crud, of course.'

'He's stuck in the crud.'

48

'Hey, that's not bad for you!' shouted Davey, elbowing him. 'Stuck in the crud! Johnny Crud and the Crudmen! The Crudbeats! Johnny and the Crudmakers. Johnny...' At that point, the bell rang and he pushed Will forward.

'Quick! Run!'

At first, Will walked home by himself after school. Davey was never ready to leave and would mess about by the class lockers, talking, wrestling, sitting on the floor endlessly packing or unpacking his bag. In the second week, though, they went along to a meeting of the Junior Debating Society ('This house believes that animals should not be sent into space') and walked home together afterwards.

'That was a laugh,' said Davey.

'I thought it was going to be deadly serious.'

'That was almost - anarchic.'

'What's anarchic?'

'Where you can say and do what you like.'

'It did get a bit out of hand. I felt sorry for old Hardshaw.'

'And sorry for the poor little animals too - those poor little monkeys.'

'Well, it's wrong, cruelty to animals. Anyway there's no need to send them now Yuri Gaga and all the others have been up there.'

'Tell you what, you should volunteer your goldfish. There's never been a goldfish in space. There's been a rat and a guinea pig...'

'Get lost.'

'We don't have a space programme, do we? You'll have to write to the Yanks. Write to NASA.'

'You're mad.'

The next week, they went again ('This house believes that "pop music" is a contradiction in terms') and afterwards walked back to their lockers where Davey had left something behind. There was no-one else around, either along the main corridor or at the lockers which were tucked away in a dead-end corner, half hidden by a stairwell. Nevertheless, Davey looked cautiously over his shoulder and lowered his voice.

'Let me show you something. This is your locker, right? And this is your crummy little padlock...'

49

'My dad gave it me.'

'Watch.'

He drew a pair of compasses out of his blazer pocket, opened them to a 90 degree angle and inserted the sharper end carefully into the keyway of Will's lock. After a few seconds of gentle probing, Will heard a soft click and saw the shackle spring open.

'There you are - piece of cake.'

'Have you been going in my locker?'

'Don't worry - I know you've got nothing in there but books, boring books.'

'I'm going to tell Mr Watts.'

'It's just a bit of fun. I never steal anything otherwise they'd start having prefect patrols or something. And I'd be under suspicion. People would say: "Oh, Farrell's always last to leave." People like you...'

And he pushed Will.

'No, I...'

'Look, watch - this is Brown's locker, right? Bum boy Brown. This one's a little bit harder...'

But after about ten seconds, the same thing happened. This time, Davey pulled open the locker door and rummaged about inside.

'Smelly gym shoes but no dirty magazines. I won't tell you what I found in here last week.'

'What?'

'No - I won't tell you. My lips are zipped. I don't steal and I don't squeal. Here, you have a go.'

It took Will longer but eventually he managed to pick his own padlock.

'There you are. So when you lose your locker keys and you desperately need something - your history books for Kenny's lesson, let's say - you know what to do.'

'But what if my compasses are in the locker?'

'Keep them in your satchel, you idiot.'

'But what if my satchel's in the locker?'

Davey put his arm around him.

'Then come to me, my boy. Come to me. I'll lend you mine. But first, you'll have to pay the idiot tax...'

Will pushed him away.

After half term, they began walking home together most evenings. Davey seemed to have lost interest in the lockers and Will never had to wait long. When the clocks were put back at the end of October, they would emerge from the building to face the glowing street lights and night time already gathering beyond them.

'And darkness was upon the face of the deep,' intoned Davey one evening as they came out of the corner tuck shop and started on their journey across town.

'The deep?'

'And God said: "Let there be light". And there was light.'

'Just like that.'

'And for my next trick, said God, I will create the heavens and the earth.'

'Woo-hoo! Thank God for that.'

'Amen.'

'Did you hear Malone in assembly the other day when the Rev said "Let us pray"?'

'Yeah, it was the way he said it - *Let's not.*'

'And then he farted.'

'No, that was Badger. I was standing right behind him.'

'Naughty Badger.'

'Yep. But we're all guilty. We shall all have to seek forgiveness from the Lord or face eternity in hell.'

'No, that's what Catholics have to do,' said Will. 'We're okay. God loves us.'

'Have you been stroking your willy, Willie?'

'Only once. Per night.'

'A likely story. Did I tell you about Brown? He took me into a toilet cubicle just before half term and showed me how quickly he could do it.'

'Ugh.'

'Dirty bastard. It went all down his cock and dripped on the floor. He didn't even have any toilet paper ready to wipe it up. I got out of there quick.'

'I don't blame you.'

'Yeah - I could have lost my...what's it called?'

'Virginity?'

51

'Nooo - what with that 'omo? No - my childlike innocence!'

'Oh yeah.'

'Hey, I wonder if the man in the bushes is going to be there?'

They only dared give a quick glance when they got to the park, but he was there - a dark presence standing in a border of trees and bushes, trousers down around his knees, upper body shrouded by leaves. They speeded up along the tarmac path to the exit gates.

'What does he do it for?' asked Will in awe.

'Dunno. He's a weirdo.'

They parted company. Will walked up the road to his parents' house and let himself in. He switched on the hall light, dumped his satchel by the coat stand and wandered into the living room. The curtains were open and there was enough light for him to cross the room to the fish tank. The pump was churning out little bubbles from one corner but the water was beginning to smell. He crouched down and gazed through the glass. Ginger had grown. His fins, especially his tail fin, were getting quite long and elaborate. As Will watched, the fish swam up to glare at him, then swished away. He followed it as it swam through an archway between the plants and squeezed behind a blue-suited diver that had been lowered into one corner. Then he saw his own face in the dark water, the brooding guarded look that it had. And then Ginger swam back across his field of view and he rapped hard on the glass with his knuckles. Immediately, the fish shot away again. Will grinned.

'Aargh! I'm dying, I'm dying...I'm dying for a shit. Can I come and use your bathroom?'

They were walking towards the park exit gates a week or so later. Davey was wiggling and gyrating on the path.

'Okay,' said Will. He knew Davey had another ten minutes to go before reaching home. But he felt uneasy.

'Good job the bogey man wasn't there, otherwise I might have shat in my pants.'

'He might still be lurking somewhere,' said Will.

They looked round at the bushes behind them.

'Yikes! Run!'

When Will let them in, Davey rushed straight up the stairs to the bathroom. Will sat in the living room for a few minutes, then went to the foot of the stairs. The bathroom door was still shut.

'Are you okay?'

There was no reply. He climbed the stairs to the landing.

'*Davey.* Are you okay?'

There was still no reply. He tried the bathroom door. It was locked. He sat down at the top of the stairs and counted silently to twenty.

'Davey. Answer me.'

There was no answer, but the door handle started to move slowly down and then slowly back up. Will watched. Again, it moved slowly down and slowly back up. A third time - slowly down and slowly back up. Will sighed.

'Look - stop messing about and come out. My parents'll be home any minute.'

The handle went slowly down and slowly back up. Will went downstairs.

'Fine,' he shouted from the hall. 'I'll tell them there's a burglar in the bathroom and they'll ring the police.'

He checked the time. In fact, it would be half an hour before his father came home. Then he heard the bolt slide back, but no other sound. When he peered from the foot of the stairs, he could see the door ajar. He climbed the stairs again and peered into the bathroom. The smell told him Davey had at least used the toilet. Across the landing, the door of the spare room was open and the light had been switched on. Davey was standing in the middle of it looking around.

'Hmm,' he said, inhaling the mustiness. 'Books.' The small space was full of books and magazines - some on shelves, others just piled in stacks on the linoleum floor.

'What are you playing at?'

'Sorry. I had a funny turn, then took a wrong turn and discovered your secret room.'

'It's my dad's science fiction collection. He buys and sells.'

'Spooky. Why does he keep the curtains drawn? Doesn't he want anyone else to know?'

Will shrugged.

'*Wine of the Dreamers, The Skylark of Space, Deliver Me From Eva, A Century of Horror, Adventures in Mutation*...wow, your dad's pretty weird, isn't he?'

'Yeah, you'd better not be here when he gets home.'

'I'll zap him with my ray gun.'

'There are some comic books in here too, somewhere.'

He pulled one out of a pile in the corner and passed it to Davey.

'*Utterly Mad*. Oh, funnee. My older brother gets this magazine to show how sophisticated he is. He doesn't understand it any more than I do. Who's GI Schmoe? Little Orphan Melvin? Americans are strange.'

He handed it back.

'Hasn't he got any, you know - alien sex books?'

'Not that I know of. He's got *Lady Chatterley's Lover*, though.'

'Where? Where?'

'Not in here. Follow me and switch the light off.'

They went downstairs. A mahogany bookcase with glass doors stood in a corner of the living room and Will pointed to the orange-spined paperback squeezed between two hardback sci-fi tomes.

'Wow. Have you read it?'

'No, he keeps this locked.'

'Locked! I can easily-'

'No, you can't. Anyway I told you - he'll be home any minute.'

'You know, thanks to me you're getting quite smart. You were dumber than Dumbo when I first met you.'

'Oh, thanks.'

'Well, not that dumb but you know what I mean. Naive. Wow, a piano! I can play the piano...'

'Is there anything you can't do?'

Davey sat down on the piano stool, lifted his rear end to flip out an imaginary pair of coat-tails, then with agonizing slowness and solemnity stretched his arms, flexed his fingers, tossed back his fringe and proceeded to grind out a version of the Flea Waltz.

'Terrific,' said Will as Davey stood and bowed. 'Even my mum can play that. Now I think it's time-'

But Davey had started sniffing.

'What is that foul smell?'

'Well it's not me,' said Will, unable to resist his role as stooge.

Davey swung round.

'Ah, the goldfish! The lovely little goldfish!'

He ran over to the tank and started to embrace it with his arms, then reeled back pretending to choke.

'It stinks!'

'Yeah, the water needs changing. We keep forgetting...'

'Doesn't the pump work?'

'Ah well, that gets switched off in the evenings 'cos its noisy. I think someone forgot to switch it back on again.'

'Oh, dear, oh dear. No wonder it's looking sorry for itself. Poor little fishee...'

'It's called Ginger, actually.'

'Hello, Ginger. Stiff upper lip, old chap. Help is on the way. Urr, look - is that poo coming out of its bum?'

'Yeah, you're probably scaring it.'

'Scaring it? I'll give it what for.'

He bent his head low over the water.

'Attennnnn-SHUN! That fish there! Left right left right left right left right - HALT! Yoooouuuu 'orrible little fish!'

By now, Ginger was shooting back and forth across the tank.

'Stop it!' shouted Will. He tried to grab Davey's arm, but was fended off.

'Hang on,' said Davey. 'Watch.'

And he blew through his cheeks sending the water rocking in choppy waves. Ginger sheltered behind the diver, but then Davey turned away.

'Oh God, that smell really is disgusting.'

Seizing his chance, Will pulled and pushed his friend towards the living room door.

'The time has come, the Walrus said, for you to piss off home.' It was a line he'd thought up a few minutes earlier.

'All right, all right. I get the message. I'm too rough. I'm an embarrassment. I live in a council slum. Your parents will be angry with you for letting me in.'

'You don't live in a council slum. You live in a bloody great mansion.'

'Tut, tut,' said Davey, straightening himself and picking up his satchel. 'Language, please.'

'Good riddance.'
'I don't care if the Duke of Edinburgh does use that word...'
'Get the hell out of here.'
'It's not suitable for my ears.'
'Au revoir.'
'Don't be surprised if my dad comes round when I tell him...'
'See you tomorrow.'
'Yeah, see you fat face! Twat face! Four eyes! Au revoir!'
And laughing Davey skipped off down the road.

'You'll get your homework done, won't you? Then you'll have the whole weekend free.'

Will sat alone in the house with his school books spread before him on the red kitchen table. It was a Friday evening and the yellow curtains were drawn against a chilly November night. The coke in the boiler was burning quietly, the clock ticked on the wall. His mother had made him some tea and then left to meet his father after work. They were going to the early evening show at the new cinema in town. So far, he had worked his way slowly through an exercise in his French primer and inscribed some new words in his blue vocabulary book. He started trying to memorise these but after a while put down his fountain pen and stood up.

It was draughty out in the hallway and he climbed the stairs quickly to the bathroom for a pee, then stared at his face in the mirrored door of the medicine cabinet. He unhooked the mirror that hung over the sink and held it so that he could see himself in profile in the other mirror. Then he opened the cabinet door and inspected its contents: a curling dust-edged roll of bandage, a tin box of sticking plasters, tubes of ointment, bottles of pills and a pair of tweezers. He helped himself to a Haliborange tablet, then closed the cabinet door and carefully prised a long glutinous bogey out of his nose with his index fingernail. After rolling this into a little ball, he flicked it deftly into the waste bin beside the toilet.

He wandered into his parents bedroom and sat down on the edge of the bed. The wardrobe doors were half open and he could see his father's best suit and one of his mother's dresses side by side. He let himself fall backward into the sunken middle of the bed and looked at the tasselled lampshade overhead. Then he rolled over onto the other side, sat up and studied himself again in the dressing table mirror. Outside, someone walked by whistling a half-familiar tune that he couldn't quite put a name to. He got up and peeped through the curtains but whoever it was had gone. He returned to the dressing table and pulled open a dainty little door in its frontage. A jumbled heap of curlers, hairnets, lipsticks and powder puffs shifted forward slightly as if alive. He shivered and shut the door. There were drops of face powder on the glass surface of the dressing table. He dipped his finger into one of them and smeared the stuff on his cheek, then hastily wiped it off.

Back downstairs in the living room, Will closed the glazed door behind him and switched on the electric fire. He took a library book from the corner shelf and sat down on the settee to read it. A couple of times, he glanced across the room at Ginger who seemed to be swimming placidly in his tank. Gradually he began to act out an idea in his mind. He put the book down and, with the fish seeming to watch through the glass, switched the fire off, switched the light off and left the room. In the hallway, he stood listening and thinking. The kitchen light was still on and there was a light shining in the porch. He went and switched them both off, then returned and waited in the dark. He had left the living room door slightly ajar and after another minute or so had lapsed, he pushed it open slowly and silently and tiptoed back into the room. Then he dropped to his knees and after a further pause, began to crawl across the carpet towards the tank. There would be just enough street light in the window bay for Ginger to see him when he leapt up in front of it shrieking madly - face distorted into a horrible grimace, arms raised, hands curved into claws. But he had got only halfway across the carpet when there was a loud splash, far louder than usual, which could mean only one thing. With heart thumping, he ran back to the light switch. There was a tiled floor in front of the radiogram, nothing to cushion its fall. But when he turned, blinking in the light, he saw the little creature writhing on the edge of the radiogram. He ran across the room, got both his hands round it and eased it into his cupped palms, feeling its body and fins slithering and flapping against his skin. Slowly, he lifted his hands over the tank and let the fish slide back into the water.

What if it jumped out again? Somewhere there was a black plastic cover which had come with the tank. Will ran into the kitchen and searched frantically through the cupboards. Where else might it be? He went out of the back door into the washhouse. There, under a dim light bulb amidst all the clutter, he found it on a shelf. Blowing and rubbing away the dust with his sleeve, he ran back to the living room and fitted the cover over the tank. It was slightly warped but would do. Ginger was swimming slowly round and round and looked briefly at Will as he bent down to peer through the glass, but then turned away.

He went back to the kitchen table, sat down before his French primer and brooded. It was silly but he'd felt more fear over that single splash than anything else he could think of, at least since the nightmares had stopped six or seven years ago. After a while, he managed to get some more homework done, but was still brooding when his parents came back from the cinema.

'Are you still sitting here? Haven't you finished yet?'

'Nearly. I had a break.'

'Have you heard what's happened?'

'No - what's happened?'

He felt confused rather than shocked as his mother told him.

'What? How do you know?'

'They interrupted the film,' she said. 'They flashed it on the screen.'

'He's dead,' said his father. 'Assassinated.'

They took their coats and scarves off. He cleared his books away while his mother made some supper, then they sat down around the television and watched it all. Somebody had been arrested. A man called Johnson was shown being sworn in as President. People were crying on the streets. No-one could believe it, not even the news readers.

He went to bed and lay awake for quite some time, thinking partly about the killing and what it might mean, but also about the splash in the dark and the fish wriggling in his hands where it shouldn't have been. And then he fell asleep and dreamt it all over again except Ginger had escaped from the tank and grown larger and was swimming in a stream that ran down the side of the street into the park. He followed it past the bushes where the man was still standing and on through the long rough grass down to the playing fields which other people were running across and then Davey passed him shouting: 'President Kennedy's coming!' and he stopped, he tried to make it all stop, because he was the only person there, the only person in the whole world who knew that something was about to happen, that something was about to go...*wrong*.

He lay awake, trying to re-assemble bits of the dream that were still floating around in his head. Outside, a bird was singing sweetly but sadly in the dawn light. After a while, he reached for his watch on the bedside table. The green hands showed 07.34. He lay there for a few minutes lost in thought, then forced himself out of bed, put his slippers on and went to the bathroom. After that, with one hand gripping the banister, he went downstairs to the silent hallway and the living room. There was no sign of Ginger as he walked over to the fish tank. Nervously, he glanced at the floor but how could the fish have jumped out of the tank again? He lifted the cover carefully and there was Ginger right in front of him, lying on one side at the surface of the water. 'Oh God,' he whispered. His heart set off on a gallop. He took a deep breath, bent forward and looked closely at the fish. Its gill was opening and closing very slowly and there still seemed to be a little gleam of light in its eye. He straightened up, went to the foot of the stairs and shouted for his mother and father. They came in their dressing gowns.

'Oh, good heavens,' his mother said when she saw the fish.

'This water stinks,' his father said. 'When did you last change it?'

'Oh, I don't know,' his mother said. 'Two or three weeks ago? It shouldn't be that bad.'

His father poked Ginger gently with his finger. The fish twitched.

'I've told you both before - it needs changing every week.'

'Well, you said yourself, Bill...it was such a palaver.'

'Look at the state of that water. Is that why someone's put the cover on it?'

'I haven't put the cover on it,' said his mother, looking at Will. He shrugged and his father poked the fish again.

'Well, it's still alive but only just. Fill up the bowl with fresh water and transfer it into that. But I wouldn't get your hopes up. It's been starved of oxygen.'

And he was right. By mid-morning, Ginger had sunk to the bottom of the bowl and his father pronounced the final verdict.

'He's had it.'

Will laid the fish in a little cardboard box that his mother found, along with a curled up plant frond which had been washed under the kitchen tap. Then he and his father buried it that afternoon in the garden border under the glossy leaves of a laurel bush. They stood at the spot for a few moments even though it was cold and overcast.

'We should have changed the water more often,' Will said. 'And I teased him too much. I kept making him jump.'

His father looked at him.

'Did you make him jump out of the tank?'

'I didn't make him. He just did it...I saved him and put him back in.'

He fought back the tears. When his father spoke, his voice had softened.

'I didn't want to tell you this at the time, but a lot of these goldfish they give away at fairgrounds don't last very long. They haven't been looked after. Ginger's probably lasted longer than most.'

Will nodded.

'And I told you a little fib about the goldfish we had when I was a lad. It wasn't the cat that got it. A white fungus grew over its gills until it couldn't breathe any more. At least, Ginger went quickly.'

They went back into the house. The daily paper was lying on the kitchen table with only one story on its front page.

'What's going to happen now?' asked Will. 'They're saying this man they've arrested has been to Russia.'

'I don't know about that. But you can't blame everything on Russia. They're gun crazy in America. Still living in the Wild West.'

'D'you think it will lead to World War III? '

'Who knows, Will. Who knows. Right now, I've got to get this boiler working again. Life must go on somehow, you know.'

Soirée

He came out of the tube station at Fulham Broadway and stood for a few moments on the pavement to get his bearings. This area was at the edge of his mental map of the city, a shadow land stuck in the U-bend of the river. He had imagined silent empty streets through which he would quickly pass to reach the border with Chelsea. Instead, other people were here, standing around like him or parading by in pairs and groups. A taxi had pulled up at the kerb and cars with glowing headlights were lining up to steer around it on the narrow roadway. Light fell across the pavement through the plate glass frontage of late shops and the smell of skewered meat hung in the air. Next to him, a girl danced like a marionette and sang a snatch of disco to her giggling friends. It was the latest incarnation of Saturday night.

He reached inside his new blue velvet jacket and pulled out the invite. His name was inscribed in copperplate at the top and beneath it the gilt lettering said: *Soirée, 18 October, 8pm, 22 Grove Walk, SW10*. Turning it over, he checked the crude map that he'd drawn after consulting the A-Z. There were two crosses - one for the pub where he was meeting Jonno, the other for Tod's house. He slipped it back inside his pocket. Across the road, the buildings were gloomy, municipal-looking and the pavement was almost clear. He edged forward around the back of the taxi, dodged the traffic to the other side and began to walk east.

The pub stood on a street corner a few hundred yards further along the road. It was busy too - a mixed crowd with both Paisley cravats and football scarves in evidence - but Jonno was not difficult to spot. Grey-suited, mildly horse-faced with long black hair, he sat at a corner table with a newspaper and almost empty glass. Will thought of creeping up on him, but there was a gap at the bar and he decided to order first. While the pints were being pulled, he looked at himself in the huge ornately-framed mirror on the back wall, unsure about the shoulder pads in his jacket. They stuck out too much, definitely. Was it because the jacket wasn't worn in yet or had he wasted good money? If he turned this way? If he turned that way? He paid and carried the glasses to the table.

'One more for the road?'

Jonno looked up.

'Will, old chap. How the devil are you?'

'Fantastic. Liberated. How's the old dump been since I left?'

'Well...' - Jonno consulted his watch - 'In the 26 and a half hours since you left, Nationwide Travel has been doing...as well as ever.' He held the new glass aloft. 'Cheers! This is my third by the way, but I'm now going to stop counting.'

'So, remind me. How do I get from...Kings Lynn to...Porthmadog on a Sunday, then?'

'Only with the most *acute* difficulty, Sir.'

'Eastbourne to Inverness?'

'Sir, you mock me. You draw attention to the sadness of my life. You gloat.'

'Why do you talk as if you've swallowed Boswell's "Life of Johnson"?'

'Who's *what*?'

'I know - Eccles-on-Sea to Ballymena. Any fucking time you like. Doesn't have to be a Sunday.'

'Four changes. Five at weekends. Thirty six and a half hours. Not counting the ferry. Quicker by balloon. Actually, Eccles-on-Sea is mostly under the sea so you start by submarine...'

'Ah, the best, the most imaginative travel advice in London. Quality stuff, mate.'

'We tell it like it ain't. There's nothing more boring than repeating accurate information over and over again.'

'Well, Monson reckons it'll all be computerised one day and you'll be replaced by robots.'

'I think I'll *be* a robot by then.'

'By the way, where the fuck are we?'

'There you have me, Sir. Never been to these parts before. I think we're in some sort of no man's land between frumpy old Fulham and - I dunno - cute...capricious...Chelsea.'

'Ah, it's good to hear your lugubrious voice again, Jonno. I've really missed it.'

'Lugubrious? How dare you, Sir? Subtly ironic, yes. Slightly posh - perhaps. But *lugubrious*...'

'Slightly posh, but not a patch on our boy Tod.'

'Ah, Tod...Three hours late today - a new record. Monson was standing in the window, hands on hips, you know - the angry manager pose - watching him cross the courtyard, expecting him to look up and see. Not a flicker. Tod just kept on walking, came in as breezy as ever with some cock and bull story about a stomach bug...started describing his leaking orifices -'

'Monson's putty in his hands. He can't get over having someone so posh, so well-connected working for him.'

'If all those stories are true... Anyway, to top it all, Tod threw him an invite for tonight's *soirée...* '

'Yeah, I noticed it's now a soirée. It was a party when he first announced it.'

'Well, it's going to be a select cultured thing, apparently. Anyway, that put Monson in a spin. He was on the phone to Mrs Monson - "bring a clean shirt in".'

'Oh, God. I won't feel like I'm getting away from the place at all.'

After ten more minutes of banter during which Will began to feel faintly bored, Jonno got up and went to the bar. He returned with two full pint glasses and set them both down before Will. When Will started to move one across the table, Jonno held up his hand.

'No, those are both for you, boyo. I've still got half a glass left. You need to catch up with me before we poodle along to this *soirée*.'

'You're just trying to get me pissed. I don't need Dutch courage to mingle with Tod and the toffs, you know.'

'I'll help you out if absolutely necessary. If you can't keep up with me, if you're not man enough to quaff -'

'Oh, all right. But I'm a man of taste and refinement - not a swiller.'

'It's just alcohol, old boy. Open the hatch and pour it down. Now's the season to be merry!'

Will took a deep draught. He wanted to get where they were going.

'The other thing is - Tod's dangled his sister in front of us.'

Jonno furrowed his brow.

'He has?'

'Yes - don't you remember, the other night? He said she's "looking for someone at the moment". And he said she's attractive...'

'Ah, yes. He also said she's crazy.'

'*Slightly* crazy.'

'Well, what's *slightly* crazy to Tod is probably stark raving bonkers to anyone else.'

'We'll find out. But I don't want to be incapable of action if she turns out to be ravishingly beautiful and open to offers.'

'Actually, from what I remember, she's his *step*-sister. That's a good thing. Just imagine if it took off, if it led to the altar. Becoming Tod's brother in law...'

'She doesn't sound like the marrying type. Anyway, wouldn't I be his brother in law twice removed or something?'

Jonno held his head in his hands.

'That's the reason we're drinking, old bean. So we don't have to think about things like that.'

Will made another major assault on his beer.

'You know, you're the only person who I ever have conversations like this with.'

'What I'm looking forward to is meeting this older woman that Tod's shagging. Do you remember him going on about the joys of older women?'

Will nodded. Jonno mused.

'I think that's where I've gone wrong,' he said.

It was a warm Indian Summery type of evening and when they left the pub a few minutes later, he decided to take the troublesome jacket off and sling it over one shoulder in the classic pose.

'Ooh, you'll catch your death of cold,' said Jonno in a Monty Python falsetto.

'I'm not sure about the jacket. Anyway, style has to come before health.'

They walked on for several hundred tedious yards along the Fulham Road, eventually turning south into the tree-lined avenue on which Tod lived. The house was halfway along, a modestly imposing semi-detached four storey place with white stucco coating on the two lower levels. The basement had ornate black metal bars protecting its windows while the attic floor looked rather squashed under a flat roof. The front garden had been paved over and turned into a parking space for a squat-looking silver car. They mounted the steps onto the white pillared porch and Jonno rang the bell. Music could be heard, footsteps on stairs, footsteps on wooden flooring and Tod's voice calling back to someone within. Then the door swung open.

'Will, dear boy. Jonathan. You made it!'

'At least you didn't say *Welcome to my humble abode*.'

'Well it's not quite as palatial as some of the houses around here, you know.'

'Yes - we've noticed.'

They stepped into the hall and handed over a bottle of wine and some cans of beer which Tod took without close inspection. On the right was a dark blue carpeted staircase and Will glanced up to see a shadow move along the wall at the top. They followed Tod into the large living room which ran the length of the house with French windows at the far end. Some kind of early classical or baroque music was piping softly through loudspeakers and Will had a general impression of being surrounded by gilt framed pictures on green walls and formal looking furniture with curved legs. He was also struck by the fact that despite the apparent buzz of voices they had heard in the hall, there weren't actually that many people there. A man was standing in front of a book-lined alcove, glass in hand, listening to a lively bespectacled woman somewhere in her thirties. Monson was at the other end of the room with a woman who Will assumed was his wife. Dotted around in between were perhaps eight or nine other people.

'Your choice of poison?' Tod waved his hand at a table on which numerous bottles and glasses were placed in neat columns. They both chose the same beer - like Tweedledum and Tweedledee thought Will. He turned back to Tod, his friend of the last three months, smartly casual in black cotton shirt over iron grey trousers, a whiff of aftershave on his handsome cheekbones.

'Nice place.'

'Early Victorian, dear boy, but with Regency style effects. My mother is responsible for the furnishing of the living room - I have to put up with that. It is her house, after all - well, it's in her name. We have to keep it in good condition and put her up whenever she comes over from Florida.'

'Is that your car outside?'

'No, dear boy, I don't engage in the rude mechanics of driving. That's my sister's car. She whizzes about town in it on her various - how shall I put it? - assignments. I walk or let myself be chauffered or even occasionally hop onto a bus with the hoi polloi, but never, dear boy, never the tube. Subterranean cattle trucks are not my style.'

Will nodded and swigged down some more beer. Somehow, in these surroundings, he felt inhibited from engaging in the usual banter. Tod raised his eyebrows and gave a little wave at the bespectacled woman across the room.

'That's Julia, my current *amour*.'

'Ah, men *do* make passes,' said Jonno.

'She's a decade or so older than me, but that's part of the attraction. Read *In Praise Of Older Women* as I've said and you'll understand.'

'So let's get this straight,' said Jonno. 'She had a devoted hubby...'

'Who she'd already deserted when we met.'

'...But now she's got you to show her a good time.'

'Now she's got me to console her, dear boy, and fulfil her desires. Of course, we're just passing ships, really. She knows that. Blown by different winds, exchanging precious gifts before we move on...'

'You're going to dump her soon, aren't you?' said Will.

'My dear boy, Julia and I are going to enjoy each others company to the fullest extent possible, but everything has its limits. We're going to live in the present, but in the full knowledge that everything changes...'

'Blah, blah,' said Jonno. 'You're going to shag her senseless for a while until you're tired of her, then push her overboard.'

'Who's to say he's not tired of her now?'

'That's true. Until your balls are tired of her...'

'What am I hearing?' asked Tod in mock exasperation. 'I'm hearing envy. I'm hearing frustration.' He looked around, then put his hand on Will's arm. 'Listen, my sister has vanished upstairs, but I'll introduce you later - both of you, of course. Right now, I have to mingle. Let me introduce you to my neighbours.' He steered them towards an adjacent couple. 'Paul and Virginia, Will and Jonno. Will worked with me at the office until yesterday, but has now officially left to become a librarian.'

"Oh, Tod,' cooed Virginia, a butterscotch blonde. 'You're not still working at that travel place, are you?'

'Certainly not. I just go in there from time to time and they give me pocket money. Excuse me for a few moments while I go and see someone.'

'So you're going to be a librarian, then,' said Paul staring impassively at them. Will did his best to stare impassively back. He saw a short thickset bespectacled man with a mane of swept back black hair and a large collared open-necked striped shirt.

'Uh huh.'

'Whereabouts?'

He asked the question as if the effort was almost too much.

'Haringey.'

'Haringey. Haringey. North London is that?'

'Yup.'

Paul sipped his martini pensively.

'Well, I suppose it's a step up from travel enquiries.'

'I hope so. What do you do?'

'Marketing.'

'Right.' Will swallowed more beer and looked around the room. He was completely unable to think of anything else to say.

'Excuse me for a moment, old bean,' murmured Jonno, patting his arm before slipping away.

'Darling, I'm just going to get some nibbles,' said Virginia rather disdainfully.

'All right, sweetie,' said Paul.

'Do you literally live next door?' asked Will in a sudden surge of inspiration. Perhaps he could stretch this out for a few minutes after all.

'Uh huh. We've got the basement and ground floor flat. The people upstairs are over there.' And he pointed to another couple in the middle of the room - the man wearing a waistcoat spangled with yellow stars, the woman in a black cocktail dress.

'Have you been here long?'

'Oh, about a year.' He yawned. 'It's a decent area.'

'I don't know it, but I wasn't entranced by Fulham Road.'

'Oh, you came that way? It is rather dull, but if you walk down to the other end of this street, you're on the Kings Road, you know? Worlds End, Chelsea...that's where it's all happening.'

'Really? I thought it had its heyday in the Sixties.'

67

'No, no...there's still a lot going on there.'

Virginia had returned with a plate of cheese straws and little round things. She listened to this last exchange with a grim, impatient face.

'Paul, darling, Vivienne's just come down. Let's go and have a word - I haven't seen her in ages.'

'Excuse me,' said Paul. And they both turned and walked away.

Will went back to the table, poured more beer into his glass and looked around the room. Jonno had ended up talking to Tod's bespectacled '*amour*' and he sauntered over to them.

'Oh you've had enough of Mr and Mrs Chelsea Set,' said Jonno.

'They walked away and left me. I'm devastated.'

'Well, this is Julia, Tod's friend. She's much *much* nicer.'

'Thank you!' said the wide-eyed smiling woman.

They shook hands and Will smiled back, partly to conceal his surprise. It wasn't so much the age of this "older woman" - she was somewhere in her late thirties - but the plain and conventional appearance which didn't seem to go with Tod's "adventurous rogue" persona. A polo-neck top, a check skirt, unflattering black-framed glasses, a kind of bouffant hairstyle...And were those rings of betrothal and marriage still on her fingers?

'Oh, you're looking at my rings,' she said brightly, holding up her left hand. 'Well, that's my engagement ring, that's my wedding ring. I'm not really sure why I don't take them off. I suppose I'd feel a bit bare without them. Or I'd feel a failure.'

'You're not a failure,' said Jonno kindly.

Julia was still staring at her hand.

'Perhaps it's my idea of revenge. I make love to other men while wearing his rings.' She laughed in a high-pitched nervous way. 'I've never thought of that before. It must be the drink talking.'

'How long have you been married?' asked Will.

'Oh, far too long,' said Julia wearily.

'You ask the most boringly obvious questions,' said Jonno.

'All right, then. Here's another. How did you meet Tod?'

'Well...I was sitting on a bench on the Embankment, believe it or not, just across from the Royal Hospital grounds - you know? - where they hold the Flower Show - anyway - feeling very sorry for myself and probably looking very sorry for myself, when he walked past. He looked at me and sort of walked on a few paces, then he

68

turned around and came and sat at the other end of the bench. He asked me if I was all right - he had such a charming and cultured voice, I was surprised. Well, I know some black people at work, but I've never really, you know, had any friends like that before. Anyway, he introduced himself, told me a little bit about his background and so on, gradually moved closer, told me I was very attractive but said I'd get worry lines if I carried on frowning. Then he asked me out to dinner.'

'The great seducer at work,' said Jonno. 'I've told her about Casanova being his great hero.'

Julia laughed.

'Well he can seduce me anytime. It's quite exciting - I was never expecting anything like it. Oh, talk of the great devil.'

Tod appeared at her side and put his arm around her waist.

'What's going on. I hope these ne'er-do-wells aren't upsetting you, my dear.'

'Well, Jonno's told me that you're writing a book which you've never mentioned to me.'

'Ah, that's because you don't read books, which is admirable in one way. The book of life is all you need.'

'And he's told me that Casanova is your hero, which I should have known.'

'He's not my hero - I am my own hero - but I do admire his memoirs, *Histoire De Ma Vie*. Which, incidentally' - he said, looking at Will - 'he wrote while he was the librarian at Duchcov Castle.'

'Well, who'd 'a thought it. Casanova - a librarian. That will inspire me.'

'He was getting old and had nowhere else to go. The Waldsteins took him in.'

'Oh, the *Waldsteins*...' said Jonno.

'He was bored rigid, though. I think you'll be bored rigid too, Will. Will's going to be a librarian,' he said to Julia.

'That's nice. So Tod, darling, what's this book about that you're writing?'

'It's...my own kind of memoir. Part fact, part fiction, part philosophy. Hard to classify, like me. You'll find out when you get your own inscribed copy.'

'It'll be called *In Praise Of Married Women*,' said Jonno.

'Oh, what a super title!' said Julia, half going along with the joke and half unsure. 'And I might be in it - how exciting! When will it be published, darling?'

'As soon as it's finished, my dear. I have connections in the literary world. One or two publishers are interested already.'

'You'll be writing it for ever,' said Will.

'No, dear boy. I've told you before. If you haven't made it by the time you're thirty, then you're never going to make it.'

'Five years to go then,' said Will.

'I know you have literary aspirations too, so you should bear that in mind.'

'Oh, I will.'

'But you must show me some of your writing, mustn't you darling?' said Julia stroking Tod's chest.

'My dear, I think we should...continue our discussions upstairs.'

'Oh, you do?'

'Yes I do. Things are settling down here. Vivienne has reappeared and can answer the door and swan around looking after people. That's my sister, by the way - I'll tell her to come over and say hello, guys.'

'Bye...' Julia gave a little wave as Tod steered her deftly away.

'Hmm,' said Jonno. 'I'm not sure Tod's the right man for her, you know.'

'You don't say? Is he the right man for any woman?'

'Hmm - I don't think she's entirely stable though. I think she'll take it hard when he moves on.'

'Well, perhaps you could be there to cushion the fall. Maybe that could be your chance.'

'We dropped enough hints though, didn't we? *Casanova. Women* - in the plural.'

'Well you dropped them. I think it's all part of your cunning strategy...'

'Hmm...'

'Oh stop saying "hmm". Stop looking as if you're deep in thought. In fact, stop thinking. Thinking's a minefield, a quagmire. A quagmire with mines in it. A quagmine. Don't think, just *act*.'

'You know what I'm thinking now,' said Jonno looking over Will's head. 'There really aren't that many people here. I thought Tod would have more friends than this.'

'Four of them are just the next door neighbours.'

'Two of them are us.'

'Two of them are Monson and his better half.'

'Maybe that's why he threw that last minute invite at Monson. Numbers were looking a bit thin.'

'Maybe that's why he invited us.'

'Nah, we were the first people he invited. We're his chums.'

'Maybe more people will turn up later when it's chucking out time in the wine bars.'

'Perhaps all his stories are true except the one about having lots of friends. Perhaps he can't make friends. Perhaps his ego, his sense of superiority, just get in the way.'

'To be fair, he's never actually claimed to have lots of friends. He just claims to know a lot of "influential" people.'

'All right - he likes to give the impression they're all friends, though. I wonder if he has a single close male friend?'

Jonno looked as if he was going to say something, but didn't.

'We're like courtiers in the retinue of a prince,' said Will. 'There to marvel at whatever he says.'

'Except we don't...'

'No, but at least we pay him some attention.'

'I *like* Tod. There's a decent guy in there somewhere under all the pretence.'

'There is...'

'He may look out for his own interests all the time, but he never tries to harm anyone else.'

'That's true. Your back is safe with him.'

'Talking of which, look out-.'

And Will turned just in time to see the approach of a black-haired, black-clothed female with a column of silver jangling bracelets around one arm and minimal make-up apart from mascara.

'Hi guys, I've been told to come and make myself known. I'm Vivienne, or Viv if you prefer.' She placed her hand on Will's arm.

'You're Will, I believe.'

'That's right.'

'And you're the infamous Jonno.'

'Good grief.'

'Don't worry, I've heard all about you - both of you - from my even more infamous step-brother.'

'All good, I trust.'

'Hmm, good enough, let's say.' She stroked Will's sleeve. 'I think you and I should get to know each other better. And as for you-' - looking directly at Jonno over her glass - 'you need to stop slouching in the corner like some sinister wallflower and start getting to know people apart from Tod's concubine.'

'My God,' said Jonno.

'Actually...' she said as if thinking aloud '...Can she really be...does she really qualify as a concubine? Isn't a concubine usually the second wife of a married man?'

'Er-'

'However, first things first...' She put her glass down on a side table and clapped her hands. 'You haven't touched the nibbles. We have gone to great lengths to provide exquisite little nibbles for our guests to soak up some of that alcohol. So' - she linked arms with both of them - 'let us trip, my pretty sweetings, over to the table and take care of that.'

'Wow!' said Will in a stage whisper. 'She knows some Shakespeare!'

'Does she?' whispered Jonno.

'I am a highly educated woman,' said Vivienne as they walked together into the back half of the living room where food was laid out on a table against the wall. Monson pretended to recoil in horror as they passed him. 'I went to a very well-known ladies college, which even you two may have heard of, and then to Cambridge. Here...help yourselves and I'll get you some more beer.'

Will picked up a gilded bone china plate from the table and helped himself to a crab cake, a small wedge of speckled cheese and some spicy crisps.

'Blimey,' said Jonno. 'She's even more pushy than Tod.'

'She is a bit overpowering.'

'She's got the hots for you, old chap. Definitely. I'd allow myself to be overpowered if I were you.'

'Hmm, she's attractive but...I'm not sure.'

'I think she wants you to eat to build up your strength.'

Monson's head loomed over Jonno's shoulder.

'I heard that.'

'Did you?'

'Better watch out - she'd eat both of you for breakfast.'

'You think so?'

'Probably be sick afterwards though.'

'You're hilarious,' said Will.

'Don't say I didn't warn you.' He turned away with rather a sour look on his face. Will raised his eyebrows at Jonno.

'Prick.'

'Indeed'.

Vivienne returned with two more glasses which she handed to them.

'You go easy, though,' she said to Will. 'I don't want you incapacitated. Too drunk to rock and roll.' She laughed, then looked around the room.

'I'm not sure whether this means Tod hasn't really got many friends or whether he's just no good at organising parties.'

'Let's be charitable and say the latter,' said Jonno.

'Could be both,' said Will.

'I see. So you two are just here for the beer, are you?'

'Oh, we love him really.'

'He makes work bearable.'

'That old fart there is the boss, I gather. Or so he thinks...' Vivienne gripped Will's shoulder and stood on tiptoes to talk softly into his ear. He was assailed by hot breath, perfume and a fabulous glimpse of breasts swaying under silk. 'I've kept away. I don't like the look of him. I think he'd have his paws all over me in no time and I'm fussy about who lays their hands on me.'

'Shall I make myself scarce?'

'Jonno, I'm sure you're very *galant* underneath that dry exterior. There must be someone in this room who'd like to get to know you. I wonder - shall I introduce you to Piers and Marcie?'

'Erm, later maybe,' said Jonno. 'I'll just join the old fart and his biddy for a while if that's alright.' And he took several steps sideways away from them. Vivienne laughed again.

73

'The old fart and his biddy. I bet he's fun, really. And what about you? Are you fun?'

'I can be.'

'Shall we go and find out?'

She took the plate off him and held his hand.

'Where shall we go?'

'Hasn't Tod given you a tour of the house? How shocking. You can bring your beer.'

Talking loudly, perhaps for the benefit of others, she pulled him through the living room into the hall.

'Well I won't bore you with the basement - that's just the kitchen and utility room - oh and a cute little conservatory full of dying plants. You've seen the ground floor. Let's go upstairs.'

'Actually, I wouldn't mind seeing-'

'What? I can't hear you.'

'Aren't we likely to run into Tod?'

'Oh he won't be up here very long. He's a fast worker.' She laughed raucously. 'Anyway, we have separate floors. This is my floor' - they had reached the landing - 'I use the back room as my bedroom because it's much quieter. Technically, the front room is a spare bedroom' - she opened the door to give him a quick look - 'though I use it sometimes as a living room when I'm entertaining. But that sofa unfolds to make a *luxurious* bed and mummy sleeps there whenever she comes over. And through there is a bathroom. Tod has the top floor. It suits his ego to be on top of everyone else, you know.'

'He's got the whole floor?'

'Yes, though honestly it's a bit cramped. He's got a bedroom and bathroom and what he calls his "study".'

'I see.'

'Shall we go in here? Come on - don't be shy.'

She held the back bedroom door open for him and he went in. At least now he knew the layout of the house, it would be simple to retreat. The double bed had a black metal frame with bars at both ends. Low lighting helped to subdue the orange walls and lent a glow to the Moroccan style hangings and curtains. There was a dressing table with mirror, a rather ornate screen in one corner, a floor to ceiling mirror against one wall and a scattering of dried

74

flowers, exotic feathers and framed photographs of primitive towns and desert landscapes. And a camera on a tripod in one corner.

'You like it?' Vivienne sat on the edge of the bed and slipped her shoes off.

'It's very tasteful.'

'Would you take your shoes off as well please. The carpet's quite expensive. In fact, it would be really helpful if you could just pop my shoes and your shoes outside the door.'

She picked up her shoes and held them out to him.

'Outside the door?'

'That's right. Like you do at the Hindu temples in India. This is my temple.'

He did as she requested. When he came back into the room, she patted the bed beside her.

'Actually, do you mind if I just use the bathroom?'

'Go right ahead. But I warn you - if you don't return, I will come looking for you.'

He held the door half-open and smiled.

'Why wouldn't I return?'

'That's my boy.'

As his piss hit the toilet bowl, he thought: *I'm not sober, I'm not drunk. She's physically attractive, but not very nice. It's just going to be a one-night stand. I'm not very good at casual liaisons, but I should be able to make it. Does my breath smell?* There were several toothbrushes in a jar. He chose one and quickly brushed his teeth.

When he returned to the bedroom, it seemed she had disappeared until her voice said - 'It's all right, I knew you'd come back. I just think it's more erotic to undress behind a screen, don't you?'. She emerged and walked straight across the room to him. Will felt immediately as if he was now in another world.

'You can take these off for me in a little while.' She patted her knickers. 'But first let's get you ready.'

'Get me ready?'

She held a finger to his lips, then began to undo the buttons of his shirt one by one. He kissed her hair, the top of her head while she was doing this. Next she took one hand at a time and undid the cuff buttons. Then she walked round behind him, pulled his shirt off and dropped it onto the floor. After that, she walked slowly back round to face him again.

'You're very systematic.'

She slapped him lightly on the cheek.

'Don't be boring. And don't try to be clever. I want you to leave your ego at the door with the shoes.'

His ego didn't like that. *Find the words - quick...*

'My ego doesn't like that idea.'

'Aaaahh.' She stroked his cheek, then leaned forward on tiptoes and kissed him lightly on the lips. Her breasts pressed briefly against his chest.

'I can't function without my ego.'

Her hand went down and stroked him.

'This tells me you can.'

'You're a cheeky little cunt.'

She stepped back and slapped his face hard.

'Would you like to say that again?'

He felt torn between picking up his shirt and walking out, or holding on for the eventual reward.

'Is this going to be love or war?'

She smiled and lowered her hand.

'You're not bad. I like you really. Now breathe in.'

She undid his belt and the top button of his trousers and slowly pulled down his zipper.

'There. You can do the rest. And please take your socks off as well. There's nothing quite so ridiculous as a naked man with socks on.'

He took the rest of his clothes off while she stood in front of him hands on hips. Then he moved forward, put his hands on her shoulders and kissed her lightly on the lips. She moved her hands to his hips, slid them around his back and they embraced. He inhaled her scent and kissed the side of her neck above and below the thin gold chain that encircled it.

'Hmm, I can feel it. Let me see it.'

He stepped back and she ran her fingers underneath his swaying cock, then lightly smacked it.

'It's rude to point.'

'You're really into slapping, aren't you?'

'Oh I'm into much worse than that.'

76

'Can't we just get into bed?'

'In a while. Haven't you heard of foreplay?'

He moved his hands to cup her breasts.

'Wait!'

'What?'

'I think we need to spice this up a bit. Let me show you my toy chest.'

At the end of the bed was a black trunk decorated with silver filigree. She lifted its lid, then looked at him and crooked a finger.

'Come on. Come and have a look.'

He went and had a look. Such a strange assortment of things lay inside the trunk that he had difficulty at first in comprehending.

'Oh what a lovely open mouth!' said Vivienne with a crooked smile. Then she picked up what appeared to be a riding crop and used it as a pointer.

'Down at the bottom here we have a saddle.'

He saw it lying upside down with straps and buckles attached. A pair of black riding boots lay across it.

'Here we have a nice pink fluffy pair of handcuffs. And here a nice shiny pair of metal handcuffs for more serious games.' She swung them from the end of the riding crop. 'A retired police sergeant gave me these.'

'Jesus!'

'Lots of rope as you can see. You can never have enough rope. Some - hmm, no. I won't tell you what those are for...I know - what about this?'

She dropped the riding crop back into the trunk and pulled out something long and purple.

'What the fuck is that?'

'You don't know what this is? Oh, sweet William. You have led a sheltered life. It's a double dildo. I call it the Equaliser.'

She held it up in front of him.

'Oh my god.'

'Look, it has a knob at each end. It's for two girls really but it can be used on men. This end goes inside me. And this end goes...here.'

She patted his bum.

'I don't think so.'

'Oh, don't worry sweetie.' She stroked his arm. 'It won't be that bad. I've got some jelly that will ease the passage. Also, it's rubber - it won't tear you or anything. You just bend over the bed, I put a couple of cushions under your tummy...'

'No way. Not my thing at all. Look I have a real knob here and it's not very happy with all this.'

He pointed to his drooping cock.

'But it's not all about *your* pleasure. There's been a revolution, don't you realise? Women want sexual pleasure now as well and this will give me what I want.'

'Well -'

'Look - ' She held him by the shoulders. 'You let me do this and then I'll let you paw my tits and do your missionary position thing or whatever it is you like doing.'

'No, I'm sorry but this is really turning me off. Not just the dildo, but everything else. Your whole attitude...'

She dropped the dildo onto the bed.

'I see. You're a coward. A boring little wanker...'

There was a pause.

'You're vile,' said Will.

He picked up his underpants as casually as possible. But then he saw a look in her face that wasn't anger or contempt, but resignation, dejection. She seemed suddenly almost vulnerable.

'Look,' he said softly. 'I have piles - it would never go up me.'

'OK, you have piles.'

'I can give you pleasure. I can give you an orgasm. I'm not selfish...'

He stepped towards her and reached out his hand, but she backed away.

'I've heard that so many times. Just - forget it.'

'Couldn't we?...'

'No. It'll take at least ten minutes to get your cock up again. And only if I act the whore or the nursemaid. I've been through it all before and it's just too tedious.'

He pulled on his jeans and socks and picked up his shirt from the floor. Vivienne slammed the trunk lid down, then walked back behind the screen. Will buttoned up his shirt.

'OK, see you later,' he said.

There was no reply. Outside, he sat on the top stair to put his shoes back on, then went down to the living room. The music had stopped and there were even fewer people around than before. In the front part of the room, Tod was holding forth to Paul and Virginia and another couple. There was no sign of Julia. In the back part of the room, Monson, his wife and Jonno were standing in front of the large windows. A woman he hadn't seen before was sitting slumped over the food table. He picked up a couple of cans of beer and joined the little group at the back.

'Greetings, squire,' said Jonno. 'You need a drink or two after your experiences upstairs?'

'I'll say.'

'Will was trapped by a man-eating female.' Jonno said by way of explanation to Monson.

'Ooh, show me the way,' said Monson. 'I expect she's still got plenty of appetite.'

'Well, she might just have room for a little 'un,' said Will.

Mrs Monson laughed.

'Touché,' she said. Her husband gave Will another sour look.

'Fortunately, this clever young man no longer works for me,' he said.

For a while, the talk was disconnected, desultory and Will thought about leaving. Vivienne had not come back down, but he felt that with so few people left, it could be awkward if she did.

'Anyone know what time the last tube is?'

'Oh you've plenty of time yet,' said Mrs Monson looking at the little watch on her wrist.

Monson was looking out of the windows and Will turned to look too. The garden was not very big and, apart from planted borders, mostly paved. In the middle, however, in a brick-lined square of soil, was a tree and under its spreading branches lay a thin scattering of brown leaves. All was illuminated by outdoor lights.

'The leaves are falling again,' said Monson. 'The end of another year coming up...'

His voice lacked its usual overbearing tone.

'Hmm,' said Will.

'You can't help thinking that time is passing you by.'

'Yep.'

'I'm fifty two. *Fifty two*. How can that be? It's frightening.'

He hiccupped. Outside, another leaf came floating down...

'Nature won't let us forget, will it? The way of all things...'

Will felt himself swaying slightly on his feet.

'Yeah yeah yeah,' he said with affected weariness. 'The leaves fall off the trees and we're all gonna die some day...'.

Monson turned and glared at him.

'Are you trying to take the piss? You think you're so fucking clever, don't you?'

Even through the beer haze, Will was taken aback by the anger and hurt in Monson's eyes.

'I wasn't taking the piss, but it's a bit of a cliched observation. Surely you haven't just realised that the leaves fall in autumn?'

'Of course I haven't just realised. But I know in *here* what it means.' Monson patted his chest. 'Not just up here.' He tapped his head. 'I know something you don't. Because I've grown up.'

'Ignore him,' said Mrs Monson to Will. 'He gets like this sometimes.'

'Do you want to know what the secret of life is? The one thing that clever young people like you don't understand?'

'Go on then.'

'It goes so fast. Faster and faster as you get older.'

Will shrugged.

'So I've heard. It's not going very fast now though.'

'You'll find out.' Monson nodded grimly over his glass. 'And you know what? It'll be an even bigger shock for you and your friends because you're so sophisticated, so knowing...'

Will opened his second can and took a sip.

'Well, I'll cope somehow. Stay forever young, Monson. That's the solution. You've allowed yourself to get old.'

Monson took a step towards him, but Mrs Monson gripped his arm.

'John, this isn't necessary. Just calm down.'

'You fucking idiot.' Monson's beer-inflamed breath swept over Will's cheek as he turned his face away. 'You're nothing. No-one. You're just a mouse inside. Just a little mouse.'

Will felt a dampness on his chest. He stepped back and looked down. Beer had splashed onto his shirt.

'Fucking hell.'

Tod's rich tones suddenly descended on them.

'Gentlemen, gentlemen. I didn't invite you here to quarrel or fight. This isn't a public house, you know.'

'That's right,' said Jonno. 'This is a *soirée*.'

'And fuck you too,' said Monson before turning away.

'Would you like a cloth, dear boy?'

'No, leave it, leave it,' said Will. He dabbed the stain with a handkerchief while looking over Tod's shoulder. There were only two people left in the front part of the room. Jonno looked too.

'Where's Julia? Where's Vivienne?' he demanded. 'The women are disappearing. It's like Bluebeard's castle for heaven's sake!'

'Julia's having a little nap. As for Vivienne, I believe Will saw her last.'

'Will? What have you done with her, you fiend!?'

Will was taking a long swig of beer.

'We're just good friends,' he muttered, but no-one was really listening.

'Tod, dear,' said Mrs Monson, who had manoeuvred her husband onto a Queen Anne chair and was now sitting on his lap. 'This may be the wine talking because I have had a glass or two, but could I possibly ask you a rather delicate question?'

'Of course, Mrs M.'

'Did you say that Vivienne is your *step*-sister?'

Tod nodded with the self-satisfaction of a man who knows that the conversation is heading into familiar waters.

'Let me delicately resolve your confusion,' he said grandly. 'She is my father's legitimate daughter.'

'Ah, I see,' said Mrs Monson, instantly enlightened.

'I am his illegitimate son. And therefore' - he paused - 'you're perfectly entitled to call me' - he lowered his voice - '*a black bastard*.'

How they laughed.

'Black bastard!' repeated Monson, shaking with glee.

'Thankfully, he decided not to disown me. And his fiancee - who I now call "mother" - thought what a splendid virile swashbuckling chap he was, impregnating one of the servants - or whatever my real mother was.'

'So you don't know who your real mother was? Or is?'

'No, not yet. My father has said he'll tell me whenever I decide that I want to know. But that will be another story, a future volume in my ongoing *oeuvre*.'

'Which the world awaits...' said Jonno.

'How interesting,' said Mrs Monson.

'Tod, I think I'm going to make a move,' said Will, patting his friend on the shoulder as he moved past him.

'Understood. Do you want me to order a taxi?'

Will shook his head.

'Actually, you could order one for us, Tod, if you don't mind,' said Mrs Monson.

Will wandered into the front room.

'Where did I put my jacket?' he asked Jonno who had followed him. They looked around the room.

'Did you take it off when you got here?'

They went into the hall. It was hanging from the coat stand.

'Oh, honestly. Of all the places to leave a coat...' said Jonno.

'Thank Christ. I thought for a moment I'd left it in Vivienne's bedroom.'

They laughed.

'No dear boy. The only thing you left there was your virginity.'

'She should be so lucky.'

'Who should?' Vivienne's voice rang out from the top of the stairs. But Tod came into the hall at that moment and called up to her.

'Vivienne, come down and mingle, my dear.'

'There are no fuckers left to mingle with.' She started walking panther-like down the stairs.

'Tod, I have to go,' said Will. 'Thanks so much for the evening.' They gripped each others hand.

'Why don't you share the Monsons' taxi - they're going to Victoria. Then you could get the tube.'

'I'd rather walk.'

'He'd rather crawl,' said Jonno.

'I'd rather ride on the Wall of Fucking Death.'

'Ooh, don't mention death to Monson,' said Jonno.

'And don't mention fucking to me,' said Vivienne loudly. She was now standing with arms folded at the foot of the stairs.

He was trying to formulate a reply, a polite but sarcastic reply, when Monson lurched into the hallway.

'There he is! Wait!' He had obviously decided that sarcasm was more befitting than anger.

Tod held out an arm to fend him off.

'See you soon. See you, Jonno.'

'Mousey! Don't go! Don't leave me.'

Will had pulled the front door open and now carefully descended the steps. There was a babble of voices behind him.

'Monson's going to need help getting down these,' he called back. Nobody seemed to hear, but then with Mrs Monson again holding her husband's arm, they moved forward to the top of the steps and watched him move away rather unsteadily along the pavement.

'He's going the wrong way,' said Jonno. 'He's going towards Worlds End. Should we stop him?'

'Let him go. I've let him go. Ponce! Librarian!' said Monson.

'He'll be fine,' said Tod. 'He'll plod along at his own pace and get there eventually.'

'He's a very bright young man,' said Mrs Monson. 'You're just jealous, John.'

'Jonno, would you like a tour of the house?' asked Vivienne.

As he neared the corner, Will glanced back at them. Why were they still standing there talking and watching him? Losers. Well, they weren't all losers. They were what he had come to expect. He lifted his arm in a farewell salute for anyone who cared to see. The Kings Road stretched away to his left. He turned to face it and began the long journey home. He never saw any of them again.

Dodgems

He took out his cigarette packet and went through the old familiar routine. Flip open the top, slide one forward and hold it towards her. Wait a few seconds... After all, she'd taken one yesterday, hadn't she? Or was it the day before? Her freckled hand had snaked towards him and...

'I've given them up,' she said. 'You ought to know why.'

He took the cigarette for himself.

'I can't read your mind,' he said.

'It's just as well, believe me.'

The contempt in her voice was pitch perfect. It was true he couldn't read her mind anymore, but it wasn't for want of trying. What did she mean - that it was bad for Lily? Even here in the great outdoors? He put the cigarette between his lips and clicked his lighter. As if on cue, a little voice piped up beside him.

'Smoking can damage your health.'

He took a first drag and looked at the packet. That's what it said, but Lily wouldn't have noticed. He imagined Maura reading it to her and Lily saying *Who is H.M. Government*? She was a good reader for her age but not the sort of curious child who studies the words around her and mouths them aloud. And nobody smoked in the books he'd read with her, but then they *were* mainly about animals.

'This is true,' he said looking down at the child on his right. 'But it also helps you think. It concentrates the mind'. And he held the cigarette aloft as if to show off its special powers.

'Lily,' said Maura. 'Why don't you come and sit on this side?'

'I'm all right, mummy.'

'It concentrates the mind so much that eventually you become wise and give it up, because...it has this unfortunate side-effect of making you ill. But I haven't reached that point yet. Of becoming wise, I mean...'

He gave her a fixed wide smile, a Joker grin, but the child looked blank.

'Why can't we *do* something?' she said.

He tapped the first stub of ash to the ground and sighed. *Why can't we do something, Lily? Because the grown-ups relationship - like the sun up there in the sky - is sinking into decline. That's why. We just sit here, your mother and I like silent prisoners sharing an invisible cell. Remember the story of Medusa in your Greek Legends picture book? The lady with black snakes in her hair? Well, this is like Medusa in reverse - your mummy turns to stone whenever I look at her...* Then he realised that his lips were moving like a fool in his own little world.

They were sitting on a bench on the brow of the common - Maura, Will and Lily - taking a break from the Easter Fair which began fifty yards away. It was late afternoon and Lily was clutching a black balloon embossed with a white skull and crossbones which floated lightly this way and that in the gentle cross breeze. Her eyes sometimes followed it, but when he glanced at her, she was staring straight ahead, just like her mother. Was she bored? Was she troubled? Her mummy and daddy had split and now mummy and her 'boyfriend' were heading the same way.

He took another drag on the cigarette, blew out some smoke and saw her daddy shambling into Maura's kitchen one Saturday last autumn. A weasel in torn denim and cracked leather, two hours late to take Lily away for the weekend. This was Rob, Maura's husband, the only other man she'd ever slept with. Rob had spoken to Maura and swept Lily off her feet, but turned his back on the new man over by the cooker, stirring the lentil soup...

He wasn't always like that, she'd told him later. That evening, in front of the fire, she'd shown him an old photograph. There they were, sitting under a tree at an open-air concert, sharing a joint in a circle of friends. Maura with long straggly hair was a less polished version of her present self, while Rob was barely recognisable with spiky hair and a street urchin's cuteness in his face that had long since disappeared.

He was an anarchist, right?

They had met in the East London Anarchists, she said, but that didn't mean a thing. She'd gone to one of their meetings with an old school friend and Rob had just drifted along in the same way. They weren't really very political. Just teenage rebels into garage rock and the Stooges and pissed off with the crap world around them. A few months later, a famous old Tory minister had rolled along to open a local fete and the anarchists gave them some eggs to throw...

We had half a dozen in a brown paper bag. Rob threw the first one and missed. I threw the next one and got him on the shoulder. Pure luck...

The police had chased and caught Rob but ignored Maura. In court, Rob pleaded guilty to disorderly conduct and got away with a fine. He emerged, chest swollen with pride, to beam at a small crowd of press reporters and anarchists.

His finest hour, said Maura. *The fraud!*

The rest of her story came out bit by bit when Lily wasn't around. How they'd moved into a squat in an empty factory where their only real possession was the mattress they'd slept on. How they'd moved on to a small flat in a rundown council block and squatted there, surviving on benefits, family food parcels, occasional cash-in-hand jobs. How their lives became so anarchic that the Anarchists drifted away and Rob made new 'friends' who wheeled and dealed. How stolen goods came to be stashed around the flat and drugs were 'tested' and sold. And as things got worse, the relationship got worse and abuse rained down on her - blows and bruises and names that hurt. Until one morning Maura was sick, and sick again the next and the morning after that. And Rob was angry until the reason became obvious and then he was fucking furious. Responsibility was being thrust upon him.

The two families rallied round and the wedding was held at Bethnal Green Register Office with a reception afterwards above a pub. She had shown him another photograph in which they stood on either side of the tiered wedding cake - haunted Maura with her convex belly and Rob with demonic red eyes, holding a vodka bottle like a weapon. Next day she awoke to see bits of icing afloat in the sick bowl beside their bed. There was no mention of a honeymoon.

After that, they were housed by the council and Rob even found some sort of job. Lily arrived on time and Rob surprised everyone by rocking her gently in his arms. And not just for the camera, but day after day, even late at night, with the voice of Otis Redding uncoiling in the background, urging him to try a little tenderness. Oh, the irony and bitterness of it! - as Maura had told the tale.

Because while Lily slept in her cot, the abuse had begun again except this time it was more intimate and cruel. She had told Will briefly and tearfully in a moment of post-coital meltdown about one of the things Rob had done to her on their bed. She had never referred to it again. Was he the only other person who knew about it? How angry she must be now at having told him such a thing.

He tilted his head back and blew a smoke ring gently towards the sky. Lily was humming a tune and bobbing the balloon on her knee. She had been four years old when Maura had packed a suitcase and told her they were going on a little holiday. While Rob was at work, they had struggled down the road to the mini-cab office and been driven to a women's refuge out in the leafy suburbs. Once safe inside the huge Victorian house, Maura had told Lily the truth and Lily had cried and cried. By early evening though, when her daddy came to the house, she had fallen fast asleep.

I left him a note. It told him exactly where I'd gone and why.

You told him the address?

Yes, because I know Rob. He'd have harassed my parents, he'd have got his nasty mates involved, he'd have claimed it was child abduction.

In fact, Rob had been so embarrassed that he'd turned up alone at the refuge. And there his access was blocked by two women of a kind he'd never met before. He had stepped back and scanned the windows of the house in vain, though Maura was watching and saw him slope away.

A few months later, Maura turned up as a temp at Will's workplace. And then it became his story as well. How they started lunching together, then going out in the evenings while her parents babysat, then spending the weekends together at her new flat in Gants Hill. And how well it had worked in the beginning, even with some of the heavy stuff going on in the background - the meetings with social services and solicitors, visits to court to get Rob to pay up. As well as acquiring a girlfriend, he had wandered into a family and there had been kids films at the local Odeon, the playground in Valentines Park, that half-term week when they'd explored museums and urban farms, fireworks in November, a trip out to Epping Forest to admire the autumn leaves and then secret shopping for Christmas...

And that was where it had started to go wrong - between Christmas and the New Year. Spending long afternoons and evenings with her family and friends, dulled by all the alcohol, he had simply dried up at times, withdrawn into himself, been no fun. And he knew it. In January, there had been impatient looks from Maura, curt remarks, a new brusqueness in bed. In February, she had moved to another job and the relationship had begun to fall apart amid the frosts of midwinter...

Of course, he had analysed it all, cigarette in hand as now. She had turned to him partly on the rebound, partly for moral support as she went through all the turmoil, and partly to signify to Rob that there was no return, the break was final, she had '*someone else*'. And then as the months went by, she realised that Rob had someone else too, that he had no intention of returning and that she was free to sort herself out and re-orientate her life. And Will - he was re-classified first as a stopgap and then as a hindrance.

I have a lot of time to make up.

And here they were in March on a fresh spring day. And what they had both seen once as the start of a new life was now a weight that only he was bothering to carry around. Why hadn't she just ended it? Was he still some use to her? Why was he still here anyway if so unwanted? Because it was all he had? Because he would otherwise be alone again? Because he would lose face with everyone he knew who thought they were still a couple? Because he would be pitied? A self-bombardment of questions.

He took a final drag from his cigarette and then something happened at last. The hand holding the burning stub flopped slightly to the right, the balloon held by Lily drifted slowly to the left and the two brushed gently against each other. The BANG made him jump and he watched with horror as a strip of shrivelled latex fell across his thigh. He brushed it away and looked at Lily. Her face was screwed up with pain and she began to cry, silently, which made it seem even worse. Maura looked at him at last.

'You idiot. Even Rob's given up smoking in front of her.'

'I'm sorry Lily,' he said, trying to keep the misery out of his voice. 'I'll get you another one.'

He stubbed the cigarette out underfoot and put his arm out to stroke her. But the child jumped down off the bench and scurried around him to her mother.

'Move down.'

He shifted along and silently cursed. Why can't children be more robust? You'd think Lily...after all she's been through - but no, he was a negligent fool. But it was impossible when the other partner...he looked at the scene in front of them. People were strolling across the grass - couples entwined, families hand-in-hand, all talking earnestly to each other, all seemingly content. And beyond them, the fun of the fair - the lights and music, the bells and sirens, the shouts and screams, the thunder of wheels on wooden boards... He waited for a minute as Lily's shaking subsided, then took a chance and stood.

'Come on, Lily,' he said. 'I'll take you on some more rides before we go. And we'll find another balloon.'

Maura ignored him but after a few seconds, Lily looked up. He raised his eyebrows, smiled at her and cocked his head towards the fair. And to his relief, the child slowly extricated herself from Maura's embrace and came towards him, holding out her hand. And although she slipped out of his grasp after the first few steps, it was only so that she could skip freely beside him as they walked down the slope towards the fair.

'Don't be too long, Lily,' Maura called after her. 'We've got other things to do'.

They went in via a little alleyway of food stalls offering burger and onions, chips, donuts and candy floss. He bought her a stick of the latter, partly as a distraction from the nearby Hook A Duck stall where she had won her balloon. He wanted to leave that for later. They went on past the Waltzer, the Ferris Wheel and the Ghost Train, then stopped while Lily clambered onto a roundabout and sat in a giant tea cup which twirled her gently from side to side. He waved to her each time she came round and she waved back. After that, when she'd finished the candy floss, he persuaded her onto a junior dipper ride in a car decorated like a bobsleigh.

90

Eventually, they reached a high steel tower with a lengthy metal arm which swung to and fro. At the end of the arm, people were strapped at the waist and shoulders into a row of seats, leaving their legs free to kick the air. The arm went higher and higher until it stood on end above the tower and then swung over to the other side, looping the loop. Lily stood beside him listening to the screams and shrieks and watching in awe as the people turned upside down in their seats. She peered at them as the ride slowed and they returned to earth, apparently none the worse for wear. Then she put her hand in his again and they walked away. Soon she was skipping ahead, pausing with fear perhaps or caution, then skipping again and singing "Red and yellow and pink and green", turning a circle and waving her arm. And indeed, every ride was decorated in bright, luminescent patterns - stripes and swirls of red and yellow, orange and yellow, purple and yellow, turquoise, pink, electric blue. And each ride had its own sound system pumping out music and messages, one of which caught his ear through the chaos...

'Come along now, take the wheel! Drive the dodgem cars, drive 'em round!'

'The dodgems!' he said to Lily. 'Shall we have a look?'

They found the rink and stood on the lowest step watching the cars cruise around before them. He kept seeing one car in particular, steered by a bald jovial man in a blue check shirt with a black-haired boy laughing and whooping beside him. They seemed almost joined at the hip in their excitement, careering around the edge of the rink, slamming against other cars and then getting into a three-car pile-up which someone had to leap in and sort out.

'What do you think?' Lily looked uncertain. She was standing close to his side.

'It'll be fine. I'll drive and we'll bump the others as much as they bump us.'

She nodded her head and he led her to the ticket booth where they bought the gold-coloured token which operated the cars.

'Can I put it in?' she asked. He gave it to her to hold. She seemed so small and fragile standing beside him that he felt a little stab of doubt, but by this time the cars had slid to a halt and there was shouting and confusion as some people extricated themselves and others swooped in.

91

'Quickly!' he shouted. Pulling her behind him, he stepped down onto the rink and hurried around anxiously as the first two or three cars were taken. Then suddenly he noticed a bright yellow car standing empty on the far side. They ran towards it and he slid into the driver's seat, while Lily clambered in beside him. There were two black seat belts. He helped with hers, then started to pull his own belt over his head but it was very tight against his chest and he didn't see how he could get his arms through it.

'How...?' He struggled a bit further, then caught the eye of a scrawny man in a red T-shirt who was weaving around the stationary cars.

'You don't need one mate,' the scrawny man shouted. "They're for the kids". And then bent over as he went by to check that Lily was secure as if this punter couldn't be trusted.

He squirmed out of the belt and tried to get comfortable. It was years since he had done anything like this and dodgems had never really been his idea of fun. He felt tense, his stomach muscles had contracted. But at the same time he knew why he was doing it. Everything had become clear. He was doing it to restore his independence and dignity. He was doing it to bolster his self-esteem. He was laying the groundwork for a graceful exit. He saw the child running wildly back to her mother, proclaiming how good it had been, how good it had been with *him*. And then later he would take Maura aside and say...

'In here.'

He pointed to the slot and Lily slipped the token into it with a cute little flourish. He would miss her. Would she be upset when he left? The music had begun blasting out again and the cars around them were slowly starting to move. He gripped the steering wheel and pressed down cautiously on the pedal. Nothing happened. He pressed down harder and still nothing happened. The cars around them were picking up speed.

'Hold tight,' he said. He braced himself and pressed down as hard as he could, hoping the car would suddenly jerk forward. It did for one second, taking them about two feet into the rink and then stopped again. 'Shit!' He pressed down hard again on the pedal but the car was completely dead. 'Fffffuc....!' He looked around in panic. The noise from the other cars threatened and the brash music from the loudspeakers pounded in his ears.

'Why won't it go?' cried Lily. Her face was pale and strained.

And then a car ran into the back of them with a bone-juddering CRASH. It was the sort of thing they'd been watching a minute or two earlier, but it felt even worse than it looked and he saw Lily's body jerk forward. She screamed and then started crying. Seconds later, another car hit them on her side, knocking them round so that they were facing the edge of the rink. Lily shrieked and he tried to get an arm round her while unbuckling her seat belt. And then, as if he'd swung down on a jungle vine, the man in the red T-shirt was standing on the bumper of the car gripping the pole and with a few strong deft movements had freed the other two cars and pushed them away.

'Out!' the man beckoned.

Will stood up and turned to Lily, but she grabbed the man's hand instead and pulled herself onto the wooden platform that ran around the rink.

'Stand by,' he heard the man say as he followed him onto the platform.

But Lily had run straight down the steps and was standing in a little clearing, sobbing wildly and looking around. People were looking at her and one or two showed concern.

'Where's mummy?' she demanded as he approached. 'I want to go back to mummy!'

He crouched down in front of her and gripped her shoulders.

'Look, we'll see mummy in a few minutes. It's okay. You haven't been hurt. The car wasn't working properly. We'll go and get our money back.'

But he was gabbling and he knew it. She pulled herself away from his grip.

'I want mummy!' she wailed. These were the worst words in the world.

'But we haven't got your balloon yet.'

He looked around for a balloon stall or a wandering vendor, but there was nothing like that in sight.

'Let's just go and find a balloon - a really good one.'

'I want mummy!' the child screamed.

He stood up. Glancing around, he could see a number of people looking their way. What were they thinking? What if they thought he was...? Time to be decisive.

'Come on, then. We'll find her.'

He put his hands in his pockets and set off without haste as if all this was perfectly normal. For the first time, he noticed the long black generator cables which snaked across the grass on their way to feed the rides. Lily trailed beside him, moaning and stumbling sometimes, her face pale and stretched, eyes flitting this way and that. He knew it would be futile to try and hold her hand. They stopped and changed direction a couple of times while he got his bearings. He was aiming for the towers of a giant bouncy castle near the entrance. When they got there, he saw Maura in the distance, still sitting on the bench with her bag beside her, but looking away from them. He started to walk up the slope without saying anything to Lily, hoping they could at least arrive together and he could throw a few words of his own into the story. But Lily saw her mother and started to run and he knew it would all be over by the time he got there. Nothing he could say would make any difference. He felt miserably depressed at what was about to happen - it all seemed so inevitable. He felt as if he were a small child himself, but motherless of course. Why didn't he just walk away? He could turn around, go back through the fairground and out the other side. He could find the station. Or he could just keep walking through the suburbs with the shackles falling away behind him and disappear into the big city. What did it matter?

But no. It was wrong to run away and it was too late. He was only about thirty yards away and could see the mother embracing the child. He could see the dramatic gestures of horror and concern. She was coming alive again with all that meant. This would be the end, but he could say a proper goodbye to Lily. He fumbled in his coat for the cigarette packet, but then left it. He could imagine the sharp glitter appearing in Maura's eyes and the dark venom gathering in her lips as he got closer. By the time he got there, she would be ready.

Forever

Fran was the pint glass, Lyn the half. Fran sat forward on the upholstered seating, Lyn sat back. Both put their glasses down carefully after supping as the little round table wobbled despite its cast iron legs. All around them, framed prints of Old London hung from the panelled walls. It was mid-week and mid-evening in the Black Horse. The quick drinkers after work had gone. The place had settled to low level conversation, the turning of newspaper pages, the gentle bubbling of a filter pump in the fish tank opposite. Fran watched the little creatures swish through the illuminated water in their wetsuits of black and gold.

'It's the only show in town,' she said dreamily.

'What?'

She pointed at the tank.

Lyn gave a scornful glance, then nodded at the door.

'Plenty of action out there. We're just off the beaten track, that's all.'

'On the dark side of town, you mean?'

'Something like that. The pub that time forgot...'

Fran looked around, picked up her glass again and drank.

'This is what purgatory will be like,' she said. 'But with no alcohol.'

'Who says you'll get into purgatory?'

'Me. I'm much too good for hell but not *quite* good enough for heaven.'

Lyn laughed.

'That's partly true.'

'I'll have to spend a few aeons in a place like this until they decide. Imagine it - just sitting here looking at the fish, talking about nothing, pacing up and down, same people every day, the bar running dry...'

She shivered.

'I don't know what you're laughing at, Sister Lynsey. You should be taking it seriously. You believe in all that crap.'

Lyn lifted her glass.

'Cheers,' she said. 'I do take it seriously.'

'Sorry,' said Fran. 'I'm not myself. I'm agitated.'

'You're totally yourself - as long as I've known you, anyway.'

After a pause, Fran went back to an earlier conversation.

'It's a classic situation, isn't it? I'm with Will, but I want Josh. I want

Josh! I want him!'

'Shhh,' said Lyn, laughing again. 'I think Josh does have a fancy for you. You might get somewhere with him, but...only on the side. He's not going to leave Susie and his comfortable house.'

'And his music collection...'

'And his lovely garden.'

Fran frowned.

'He's definitely interested...I can tell. Has he said anything to you?'

'No, but you know how tight-lipped he is.'

'Bastard...I love him.'

'I do get little signals, though...sometimes. It's hard to pin down.'

'He wants me.'

'I could be imagining it.'

'You? Imagine something?'

'This beer will be going over your beautiful head in a minute. How *is* Will-o'-the-wisp, by the way?'

'Will? The *ignis fatuus*? He's okay. Same as ever. I am getting a teeny-weeny bit fed up with him. Beard hairs in the bathroom sink again this morning.'

'Oh, no. He just wants to share his masculinity with you...'

'There are other ways he can do that. Have you heard anymore from-?'

'No.'

Lyn's long white fingers gripped the glass as she took another sip of beer.

'Oh...I see.'

'I don't know anyone of that name.'

'Fair enough.'

Fran gazed at the fish tank again and crooned softly.

'What can a poor girl *do*, de-deh deh-deh - whoops!'

Her knee had knocked a table leg and their beer rocked dangerously.

'I'm reading Marquez,' said Lyn brightly. 'A Hundred Years of Solitude. It's good once you get into it.'

'Told you.'

'Better than that other book you recommended - the flipping French Lieutenant's Woman.'

'Oh that's good, too. I love Fowles. You should see the film.'

'I wouldn't mind seeing the film. I missed it when it came out. A certain moron whose name escapes me wouldn't go.'

'Well, there you are then. You're better off without him.'

'I like Meryl Streep.'

'Sophie's Choice.'

'Manhattan.'

'Oh yeah, Manhattan. I'd forgotten she was in that.'

'My ex-wife left me for another woman.'

'Yeah, but that was Woody's film. She's only a bit player in that one.'

'True...'

'How about the Scratch Messiah concert, then?' said Lyn. 'Are you up for it?'

'When is it?'

'First Sunday in December.'

'Will I have to sing?'

'No, there'll be three thousand people in the choir.'

'Three thousand people?!'

'At least. You'll love it.'

'And do they admit atheists?'

'They do - they're not fussy. They'll admit anyone who's bought a ticket. All proceeds in aid of the British Heart Foundation.'

'Yes but isn't the music supposed to glorify God?'

'It does.'

'Hmmm...but does it transcend religious belief?'

'Oh for...God's sake!'

'Oh all right. I'll come along.'

'I'm going anyway. I've gone for the last three years.'

'Well this year, baby, I'll be right there with you.'

'That's more like it!'

'Cheers!'

They clinked their glasses and drank.

'One more for the road?'

Lyn shook her head. After a while, they put their coats on, picked up their bags and threaded their way between tables and stools towards the door. A good night wave to the bar person and they stepped out into the gloom of Rathbone Place with its feeble street lamps, grey brick facades and shuttered shop windows.

'Let us go then, you and I' said Fran as soon as the door shut behind them.

'Oh, do we have to?'

'Ye-es, come on!'

Lyn glanced upward, then responded.

'*When the evening is spread out against the sky...*'

'*Like a patient etherised upon a table.*' This was chanted together as they set off down the street.

'*Let us go through certain half-deserted streets...*' said Fran with a wave of her arm.

'*The muttering retreats...*'

'*Of restless nights in one night cheap hotels...*'

'*And sawdust restaurants with oyster shells...*'

'*Streets that follow like a tedious...argument...*'

'Er...' said Lyn.

'*Of insidious intent...*' said Fran.

'Er...'

'*To...* something or other' said Fran.

'Oh...*to lead you to an overwhelming question*!' cried Lyn.

'Oh, yes. *Oh, do not ask, 'What is it?*' ' said Fran.

'*Let us go and make our visit*!' they chorused.

They stopped at the corner and faced each other.

'I'm fired up now and we're going home,' said Fran. 'Let's do something. The night is young. Let's make our visit to a lap dancing club.'

Lyn laughed.

'You are funny. Another time. I'll come and watch you.'

'It'll be better than the bloody Messiah.'

'I'll get you a ticket. You'll love it. You love high art.'

'High art? Give me a high five!'

And Lyn did so, albeit embarrassed. Then one went east and the other went west along the gaudy wastes of Oxford Street. And the one who went east, still infused with beer and poetry, said to herself: 'Good night, sweet ladies. Good night, good night' as the big red buses went lumbering by.

A few weeks later on a Sunday evening, they met in front of the newspaper kiosk at South Kensington tube and headed for the side steps that led down into the long pedestrian tunnel.

'I love this tunnel,' said Fran as they rounded the bend and saw it stretching ahead.

'Hmm - it gets a bit boring after about...ten seconds.'

'There's usually a good busker. The acoustics are good.'

But no-one was busking that evening and after the first fifty yards or so, Fran did begin to feel mildly claustrophobic. Advertising posters broke up the monotony of the brown and white tiled walls but other people were walking the same way close in front and close behind and a general hubbub of voices reverberated under the low ceiling.

'Are we late? Why's everyone hurrying?'

'They just can't wait to get there,' said Lyn dryly. She wasn't talking much.

'Left,' said Fran. 'Left. Left right left.'

At the end, they climbed the steps that led onto Exhibition Road and walked a little more freely past Imperial College and up the crescent of Kensington Gore. Halfway along, part of the famous red brick rotunda came into view. Groups of people were standing around outside the various entrances, presumably waiting for friends to arrive. Fran followed Lyn through the crowd straight to Door 4 where a man in a full-length commissionaire's coat checked their tickets.

'Straight up the stairs to the top.'

They crossed the lobby, walked up the stairs as instructed and came out into a curving, red-carpeted corridor where Fran bought a programme. From there, Lyn led them to door T where their tickets were checked again and they were pointed in the direction of their seats. For a few moments, they paused on the edge of the balcony and looked across at the panoply of organ pipes and down at the interior of the Hall. At ground level, the orchestra seats and stands were placed right in the centre of the circular arena. Around them, the stalls sloped back and then the dark red tiers of seats and curtained loggia boxes rose one above the other almost to the ceiling.

'See the colour coding system I was telling you about? The altos sit on that side and wear something red. The sopranos sit on that side and wear something blue. The men sit in between and wear boring grey suits.'

Fran was still absorbing it all and could only nod. They turned and climbed the steep aisle to their seats, taking off their coats before settling down. Fran looked up at the dome. Above a suspended platform of spotlights, a number of strange circular discs were hanging from the ceiling.

'What are the flying saucers for?' she asked.

Lyn smiled.

'Everybody calls them that. I think they're there to reduce the echo

99

effect.'

The seats around them filled up. There was applause as the orchestra members came out to take their seats, more applause as the soloists appeared and applause topped with cheers as the conductor marched out in his white jacket and mounted the podium. A man in a dinner jacket stood and made an introductory speech. Then, without any dimming of lights, the music began. Some of it was well known to Fran, not only through old school concerts but because her father had always played a recording of the 'highlights' on Christmas Day. She missed that now, suddenly. Perhaps she could find the tape...

Down below, the tenor was weaving his way through the long coloraturas of 'Every Valley Shall Be Exalted' and Fran smiled at the memory of a blushing sixth form boy attempting to do the same. It felt like a long time ago. Then they reached 'And the Glory of the Lord' and everyone in the chorus rose to their feet and started to sing - first the altos, then the sopranos, then the tenors and basses until three thousand voices resounded through the hall. And every so often came a ripple of white paper along each row as three thousand score sheets were turned. It was magnificent, both as sound and spectacle, and Fran was so pleased she had come. A little later they reached her favourite chorus - 'For Unto Us A Child Is Born' - and she felt almost ecstatic as the chorus blasted out those pinnacle notes:

won!-derful mar!-vellous almighty God! the ever-lasting! Father!

The second time around she mouthed the words herself. Then gazing upward, she had a mad momentary vision of the dome above slowly sliding open and a sign appearing in the starlit sky, a divine response to this great human effort.

'Brilliant!' she whispered to Lyn.

'Told you!'

The next highlight was 'Glory To God' and then after some rather lengthy arias by the alto and soprano soloists, they reached the break.

'Shall we brave the bar?'

'Loo first,' said Fran.

But by the time they got through the exit, the loo queue was already out of the door and along the corridor. They went to the bar which was not quite as full as expected and managed to get glasses of white wine. Fran drank hers quickly and returned to the loo queue which seemed to

100

have got even longer. By the time she had finished and returned to the auditorium, the music had already started and she had to squeeze past people who would only pull in their knees.

The second half was not as exciting as the first, except for 'All We Like Sheep' which always made Fran and Lyn smile with its hint of a fondness for woolly ruminants. After that, there were many arias and recitatives that Fran was not familiar with and her attention wandered. At one point, she leaned forward and watched the very serious man in the row below who was holding a well-worn edition of the musical score and following every note, his finger moving along the page under the stave. How strange, she thought sitting back again, that all this glorious music and the great glowing spectacle in front of her were chained to a belief system that so many people had abandoned. The commitment, the fervour, the faith that all these sensible-looking people seemed to possess, that made them look so happy as they sang, was devoted to an elaborate myth spun by a Galilean cult leader as Will had once put it. It was a combined effort of mass self-delusion. Or were some of them just there for the music? But how could you sing those words insincerely? *Wonderful, counsellor, almighty God*...She shook her head. She had never thought about it like that before but the art, the 'high culture' was helping to keep a dying religion alive as if it were a life support system.

She stayed sunk in her thoughts until the start of the Hallelujah Chorus when for some reason everybody got to their feet. Lyn smiled down at her and after a few seconds of hesitation, Fran stood too. It was impossible to see anything otherwise. Once again the Hallelujahs shot out of three thousand throats like musical cannon fire and once again Fran was roused to admiration. But then she became aware of something else. What *was* the chorus singing? 'And he shall reign forever and ever...and he shall reign forever and ever...and he shall reign forever and...'

Forever

Something was starting to seep through her, a special kind of fear that she had known before. She stood frowning and furrowed, neck muscles tensed, stomach muscles gripped as if to fend it off. *And he shall reign... Forever.* Something that goes on and on and on without *ever* coming to an end. And it isn't life. *Halle-lujah!* The only thing that lasts forever, that will go on and on and on through black infinity in *endless* space and time is...*Halle-lujah!* Death after life, non-being. But how can non-being last if it doesn't exist? She had seen her father or what had been her father and kissed his brow and felt his skull on her lips...*Hallelujah!* Her heart was thumping...*Hallelujah!* Panic was spreading through her ribs... *Hallelujah! Halleluuuuuu-jaaaaaah.* To lose consciousness never to wake ever again... And suddenly there was applause and then she became aware that everyone else was sitting down. The auditorium swayed in front of her. She felt Lyn's knuckles rap her leg and turned to grip the back of her seat.

'I've got to get out for a while,' she whispered. Lyn looked at her in a puzzled way but stood up again to let her pass.

'Are you all right?'

Fran nodded grimly and moved forward. People pulled their legs in again and then she was on the steeply banked aisle, clutching for the rail at the side like an old woman. Oh God, could she make it to the exit? A deep breath, descending step by step, feeling the sweat on her brow, turning without looking aside, a few more paces and then she was there, pushing through the swing door into the cool corridor. And just after the door closed behind her, the strings started again. '*I know that my redeemer liveth*' - audible but distant like something known, but left behind. She leant against the wall and smiled weakly both at the poignancy and the irony of it. Such a beautiful melody, such a beautiful voice...She breathed deeply and breathed again and began to gain some strength. And then the door opened and Lyn came out and stood in front of her.

'What's wrong?' she said softly.

'Nothing. I just had a nasty turn. What are you doing here? This is your favourite aria.'

'It is. It's so beautiful it moved me to come out here and make sure you were all right.'

Fran pressed her lips together and clenched her stomach muscles as you do sometimes when trying to control yourself. And silently Lyn put her arms around her which she had never done before. They were capable confident women, not girly girls. They might pat or even stroke, but they didn't hug or cling. Humour was the way they dealt with things. Gently, Fran pulled away and took another deep breath.

'I've had one of those episodes...where you think about what mortality really means. I've often thought about it before but never quite like that. It was that word *'forever'* in the wretched Hallelujah Chorus...How can time just go on and on without you? No that's silly - of course it can. What I mean is - life ends but death doesn't. I just don't understand how time can be completely limitless...although, on the other hand, how it can end? An ending can only take place in time. Don't you ever think about these things?'

'No,' said Lyn. 'I think that in the next life, time stands still.'

'That's more or less the same thing as it going on for ever,' said Fran. 'Except you believe there is a next life and I don't.'

Lyn shrugged.

'Either way, it's best not to think about it too much,' she said. 'What's the point?'

She lifted her arms again and held Fran's shoulders.

'Whatever way you look at it, there's still a lot of mystery about life and human existence. You won't get to the bottom of it. The best scientists in the world don't understand it yet. There's no proof of anything. I don't say "I know" there's a God and life after death. I say that I believe.'

'But people talk about "forever" as if it just means a long time. It doesn't. It means *never ending* time with no outcome, no conclusion, no way back *ever.*'

'Well it's up to you, really, what you believe...I suppose the most you can say is that if you're right and I'm wrong, neither of us will know anything about it. Anyway, I can't believe we came to listen to the Messiah and we're standing here discussing death and eternity.'

Fran smiled.

'Will likes to quote somebody, one of the Greek philosophers I think, who said you'll end up "next door to madness" if you try and work it all out.'

'Well there you are, then. For once I agree with Will. Or this Greek philosopher, whoever he was.'

'Do you want to go back in? I'll feel a bit silly. I might just wait for you down in the foyer'.

'No, it's nearly over. We've heard all the best bits - apart from the final Amen. Let's go now and avoid the crush at the end.'

And so they went through the double doors, which shut off the music altogether, and descended the staircase. In the foyer, an impassive attendant held the final door open and the sound of traffic on Kensington Road eased them back into the real world. Fran glanced across to Hyde Park and the monument to a dead prince whose effigy sat illuminated but shrunken in its dark centre.

'Isn't the Hall supposed to be a memorial to Victoria's hubby, as well,' she said as they turned down Kensington Gore.

'Well, yes. That's why it's called the Albert Hall.'

'Duh...But you know what I mean. They're both part of the same expression of her grief.'

'Perhaps you sensed it in there.' She nodded back at the Hall. 'Perhaps that's why-'

'I doubt it. I'm not very receptive to contact from the other side.'

'But *there's* someone who was affected by death - the widow of Windsor. She wore black for the rest of her life...'

'I know. Unbelievable.'

'Actually, we owe this whole area to Albert. He persuaded them to buy the land. He had this plan for it to be a kind of cultural and scientific campus which is more or less what's happened.'

'Wow. Really?'

'Yep. You could say the whole area is a memorial to him. The cynics called it 'Albertopolis.'

They laughed.

'But that was before he died, of course. Everybody had to toe the line and be respectful after that.'

'Albertopolis,' repeated Fran. 'What a great name. I expect they'll name an area after me eventually. Franopolis...'

'That's more like it!'

'Franopolis will be an area devoted to poetry bookshops, art galleries, music clubs, funky little market stalls selling handcrafted...thingies, wholefood cafés and lots of real ale pubs and bars...'

'No churches, of course...'

'There'll be room for one old church and a Buddhist temple and a yoga centre - in fact, there'll be a sort of spiritual exploration quarter...'

'Roll up, roll up. Get your mumbo-jumbo here...'

'And at the entrances to Franopolis - because obviously there'll be more than one - there'll be big signs that say' - she drew a picture in the air with her hand - "No Cynics, No Closed Minds".'

'And in smaller letters: "Please Leave Your Brain at the Cloakroom". Look, here's the tunnel. Tell you what - let's skip it. Let's stay above ground.'

'Yes, let's. I'm in no mood for the tunnel.'

And so they walked on past the great museums, past the lawn behind black railings, across Cromwell Road at the traffic lights, past the row of cafés and restaurants with their colourful awnings to the very beginning of Exhibition Road and round into Thurloe Street and the tube. In the ticket hall, Fran gave Lyn a brief hug.

'Thanks for your patience.'

'You're welcome. Are you sure you'll be all right?'

'I'll be fine. It was just one of those existential crises that we explorers and intellectuals have to put up with.'

'Well, someone has to do it.'

'It was a lovely evening, by the way. I may never be able to listen to The Messiah again, but it was a lovely evening.'

'Nah, you'll have forgotten all about it by tomorrow. Your crisis, I mean.'

'Until the next time...'

Fran went through the ticket barrier and down the steps to the open air platforms of the District and Circle Line. There were three minutes indicated before the next train. She wandered along the platform past clusters of other people until she was alone close to the edge. Rather hesitantly, she looked up but little could be seen that evening from where she stood. No moon, no stars, no etherised patient, not even the vast black void beyond - just light pollution and the grey shapes of old buildings that seemed to lean inward as they rose beside the track. She walked across to the other side but it was the same. Frustrated, she stood and waited like everyone else for the train that would take her home. Back to the flat, its familiar rooms, the kitchen for hot chocolate, the living room for late night television, the dazzling bathroom, the dark cave of the bedroom...Back to Will who woke in panic sometimes if a siren pierced his dreams. Somehow, she felt fonder of him now.

Men and Woman

The living room curtains had been drawn for three hours already when Bob stepped to the window and pulled them cautiously apart. What was it like outside? That was the question. A few raindrops still clung to the glass, but the wind had ceased and the street was calm and quiet even with that woman's heels clacking on the pavement. A lorry swept by, followed by one car and another, headlights glowing, tyres swishing on the wet tarmac - the street was a rat run at times. But after they had gone, the evening silence seemed only to deepen and nothing affected that crescent moon balancing on an invisible point in the night sky. Was it waxing or waning? *It fills with light from the right,* someone had once said. But - *oops!* He'd been *seen.* A man walking by on the other side of the road was looking across. Bob let the curtains fall back and smoothed them into place.

'Not my type,' he said to himself. 'Anyway, I'm spoken for.' And he raised his eyebrows in mild astonishment before bending to switch off the television. He and Charlie had taken the Christmas decorations down that afternoon and although there was a big new calendar in one of the alcoves, the living room seemed a little sad and depleted now that its old familiar look had been restored. He wandered into the centre of the room and stared at himself in the gilt framed mirror that hung over the fireplace. The lights were dimmed and he had to admit that it made a difference. The lines on his brow were more or less invisible, the thinning hair seemed to have bounced back a little. The black-framed spectacles that he'd started wearing a few months ago looked natural against his pale face. The good looks were still there even if not so reliable, so *stable,* as in the past. He ran a hand over his freshly shaven chin. *Perhaps a splash more cologne?* He turned around with that thought in mind, then walked into the hall and said loudly-

'Well, at least it's stopped raining.'

But even as he spoke, he remembered that Charlie had gone upstairs.

'Does he ever turn any lights out? No.'

He walked down the narrow stretch of hallway that led to the kitchen. One of the brightly-ringed 'His and His' mugs stood on the pine table. He checked that the back door was locked, put a few plates away, wiped down the work surfaces around the sink, then lifted the mug and held it aloft in a toast apparently addressed to the white-plated boiler.

'Cheers, Charlie. You do think of some things.'

A deep suave voice came back at him from the hall.

'Talking to yourself again, eh? Time to make that appointment.'

Charlie was halfway down the stairs, leaning over the banister, smiling. He was bear-like in stature with dark ginger hair and a well-clipped beard. He was also calmly and comfortably naked.

'Ooh, you nearly made me spill my tea. Are those? - oh my God. What are you creeping about like that for?'

'I'm not creeping but it's hard to make a lot of noise when you're unclad.'

'Exhibitionist!'

'Actually, I'm just looking for the cologne.'

'Well that's pure telepathy. I want more of that. I thought I'd left it in the bathroom.'

'No sign of it, old bean. Don't worry, I'll have another look in the bedroom.'

He headed back upstairs.

'May I remind you...' said Bob, moving forward into the hallway '...that we're supposed to be there by eight pm. It's now twenty nine minutes past seven.' He held out his watch arm and tapped the glass with a fingernail.

'Well, it's only a ten minute drive, isn't it,' said Charlie looking down over the top banister.

'You forget that we've got to negotiate the perils of the one-way system. And find a parking space.'

'Oh, the horror! The horror!'

He padded off along the carpeted landing and Bob sat down on the second stair to sip more tea. The front door with its glass flower panels was straight ahead and he watched a shadow or two glide past and listened to more clacking heels and voices that weren't quite clear enough to understand.

'Found it,' sang Charlie from above. Bob didn't move for a while, lulled into reverie. Then he forced himself to stand, took the mug back to the kitchen and returned to the living room. He would have one more go at hurrying Charlie, but first he would phone Clare. He picked up the handset and pressed the stored number. After five rings, someone answered.

'Oh, hello Steve, it's Bob. Yes. Absolutely. Happy New Year to you! I was just calling to say we are *almost* ready to depart. Yes, of course....Hello? Clare! Darling! How are things? Oh good. Listen, I was just ringing to *reassure you* that we're almost - *almost* - on our way. Yes. Well you know what Charlie's like - endlessly preening himself as usual. God knows why because the only attractive man there will be Steve and he's spoken for. Well, I should hope so. You're too kind. Anyway, we'll be leaving any minute. *Any minute*. All right? Definitely be with you by eight. All right? See you soooon...'

He called up to Charlie:

'That was Clare. She said if we don't get there pronto, our dinner will be in the oven.'

'I'm coming,' Charlie retorted in a mock-irascible voice. A couple of minutes later, he walked slowly down the stairs in a tan suit with an open-necked brown shirt underneath.

'I have to admit you do look good,' said Bob.

'Listen, you old fart. I do all this *preening* for you, nobody else.'

'Oh, you heard that bit, then?'

'Heard it? I should think they heard it next door. On both sides. Here - isn't this what you wanted?'

He held out a bottle of cologne.

'Oh sugar, I'd forgotten about that.'

Bob scurried over to the mirror and began to pat some around his neck and on his cheeks.

'Now who's holding us up?' said Charlie.

He came alongside Bob and started adjusting his shirt collar.

'I like this mirror,' he said. 'It's friendly. It's on my side.'

'Yes I was thinking that as well. Much friendlier than the bathroom mirror.'

'Oh the bathroom mirror - well that's your fault. If you'd just stop shaving, we could get rid of it.'

'I think one bristly chin is enough - don't you?'

Charlie gave him a bristly kiss on the cheek, then they put their coats on in the hallway and Bob set the burglar alarm while Charlie opened the front door.

'Do you know,' said Charlie, raising his voice as the alarm beeped loudly in their eardrums. 'I was in a building the other day and I got into the lift and not only were all the walls mirrored but the bloody ceiling was a mirror too! Can you believe it?'

'Don't get me started on lifts.'

'I very nearly hit the emergency button.'

109

'Who's driving then? Me as usual?'

'I'll drive there,' said Charlie. 'You know I can't be trusted once the bottles are uncorked.'

'The wine!' screeched Bob on the pavement. 'We forgot the bloody wine.'

He turned back and fumbled with his keys on the doorstep.

'And the central heating! What should I do - leave it on?'

Charlie shrugged.

'It's up to you,' he said blandly. 'I hope to have the warm glow of alcohol in my veins when we return.'

'I'd quite like to drink as well, you know.'

'Taxi?'

'Too bloody late now.'

Minutes later, they pulled away. Across the road, a curtain fell neatly back into place.

'Here, look.'

'Yes, I can see,' said Charlie. 'Why do motor cycles have to take up so much room?'

'Be careful you don't hit the back wheel.'

'Mother of God, I would never have thought of that.'

By some miracle, they had found a parking space only fifty yards from their destination. The street was quieter than theirs. The houses were similar two-storey terraced, but with bay windows and a predominance of blinds and shutters. The little front gardens featured costly-looking potted plants that squatted on tasteful paving stones. Ivy grew around the arched doorway of Steve and Clare's and had spread upwards to their bedroom window sill. The bell chimed loud and clear inside the house. Steve answered the door.

'Is this your escape route, old chap?' said Charlie pointing up at the dark green plant.

Steve gave a puzzled smile and came out to look.

'Oh, I see what you mean. Not sure it would bear my weight.'

'Well Bob can test it for you if you like. No good me trying.'

'Take no notice, Steve,' said Bob. 'Stick to the knotted sheets.'

'Okay,' said Steve. He retained the puzzled smile as he ushered them into the house but his handshake was firm. To Bob, he still had the boyishness of a university sports hero, all white teeth and glossy black hair and chest hairs piling up beneath the open-necked blue shirt.

110

'How is she?'

'She's fine. Absolutely fine.'

And there she was, calling to them from the kitchen, eyes shining under a fringe of black hair, demure in a loose blue dress that still failed to conceal the bump, at least from the side. After a flurry of "darlings" and hugs, coats were taken, gin and tonics handed out and plates of nibbles nudged towards them as they sat down at the kitchen table. The Eurythmics played softly through speakers.

'Something smells good,' said Charlie, nodding at the cooker.

'I hope so. You'll have to excuse any splatters on the dress. It looks ridiculous when I try and tie an apron around this.'

'You look fantastic. Good Christmas?'

'We had a super-duper Christmas,' said Clare. 'We went to Steve's parents in Roehampton on Christmas Day and my parents on Boxing Day, so - no cooking required and I was fussed over from start to finish.'

'And I did a lot of very strenuous dishwasher loading,' said Steve.

'Good for the biceps, Steve.'

'How about you?'

'We had a - what?' said Charlie, looking at Bob. 'Nice quiet Christmas I suppose...'

'Our neighbours came in for drinkie-poos on Christmas morning - the nice neighbours, that is,' said Bob. 'And Lottie came round as usual for Christmas dinner in the afternoon. She was a hoot - got drunker and drunker until she fell asleep.'

'Snored through *Wonderful Life*.'

'When she woke up, we tried playing Charades, but Lottie was hopeless.'

'We got drunker and drunker and can't remember anything else.'

'Boxing Day was a day of reckoning.'

'The hangover from hell.'

'Cold turkey and bubble and squeak.'

'We did get to the opera though, didn't we - on the next day?'

'Oh, yes - *La Boheme*. Rather jaded production, I thought. Or maybe it was me.'

'And a party on New Year's Eve. That was fun. We'd only been there five minutes when a fight broke out.'

'Nothing to do with us.'

'Then somebody collapsed in a drunken stupor.'

'Then somebody banged on the front door complaining about the noise.'

'And the neighbours had been invited but they got into a huff and left.'

'*Didn't realise it was going to be like this,*' Charlie mocked in falsetto.

'Lots of horseplay in the back garden, if you know what I mean.'

'Stop - please stop,' cried Clare holding her front.

'Oh sorry, we weren't trying to induce labour.'

'You should have us in the ward when the baby's due.'

'So how did you get home?'

'Oh it was only up the road. B&B - Bernard and Bruce. You've probably met them sometime.'

'Have we met them, darling?' asked Steve.

'I think so.'

'Yes you have.'

'Don't know where, don't know whennnn...' sang Charlie in a quavering voice.

'They remember you, Steve. In fact, they asked to be remembered to you, especially.'

'Oh' said Steve, looking puzzled again. 'That's nice.'

'He's making it up,' said Charlie.

'Don't take any notice of them, Stevie darling,' said Clare giving him a hug. 'They're mischievous little buggers.'

'Oh, well - she's got you to a T, Charlie,' said Bob.

'Me? Little?'

'So you're getting all geared up for the wedding then?'

'Well, sort of. Steve's parents are insisting on sending out formal invitations which normally would be a bit late, but luckily everyone we want to come knows the date anyway. The Pattisons, Tim and Andrea, Steve's best man Sean, Will and his new girlfriend Pattie, you two - obviously.'

'I didn't know Will had a new girlfriend?'

'Yes and they seem to be getting on extremely well. I think this one might last.'

'Oh good. So no chance of changing it to Valentine's Day, then?'

'Bob, we've been through this before: (a) Valentine's Day is on a Tuesday which is no good to anyone; (b) the idea is as corny as...whatever.'

'Kansas in August,' said Charlie.

'What's corny about Kansas in August?'

'They grow lots of corn there, you idiot.'
'And the sooner we have the ceremony the better,' said Steve. 'For obvious reasons.'
'Very obvious. So how is the little one? Still kicking, I hope?'
'Oh, yes. Every now and again.'
'Can I?'
'Go on then.' And she stood in front of Bob while he placed his hand tentatively on the bump.
'Not a thing.'
'No, it's quiet at the moment.'
'It knows you two are here,' said Steve. Charlie pulled a sad face.
'It's all right, little baby,' he cooed. 'We're nice guys.'
'You've felt it then, Steve?'
'Oh yes. Lots. Definitely going to be a rugger player.'
'But you don't know the sex, yet. Are you going to ask?'
Clare shook her head.
'Girls can play rugby, you know,' said Steve.
'Absolutely,' said Charlie. 'That's put *you* in your place, Master Bob.'
'Ah, well...what would *I* know about girls?'

They ate an absolutely brilliant chicken curry made with butternut squash, sweet potatoes and lemongrass that Clare had learnt to cook during her time as a volunteer in Africa. The dessert was a superb homemade black cherry yogurt. They had honestly never tasted food as good for ages and conversation slowed while they ate until Clare mentioned how she had once in Zambia - not wishing to be impolite, but secretly 'horrified' - eaten a gazelle curry. That led them on to talk about the various exotic animals that they had eaten at one time or another, the ethics of such and the pros and cons of vegetarianism, veganism and fruitarianism. Charlie pointed out all the different types of fruit that could be consumed with or as part of alcoholic drinks. Then Bob filled Clare in on all the gossip from work since she had left in mid-December. Towards the end of the meal, Clare lit a carefully shaped Amaretti wrapper and they watched as it flamed and shrivelled and flew towards the ceiling.
'Quite an expert, aren't you darling?'
'I'm sober. Do you want a go?'
'You know mine never work.'
'They don't go in for that sort of thing at the rugger club,' said Bob.

113

Clare pushed the matches towards him.

'You have a go then, smarty-pants.'

'Ooh, I'm no good at it either. I'll probably burn a hole in your table cloth.'

'How much have you had to drink? Do you want some coffee?'

'I'd better have some coffee. I've had that large gin Steve forced on me and two glasses of wine.'

'You devil,' said Charlie. He took a wrapper and set it up rather clumsily on the table.

'Let me have a go. I like setting things on fire.'

His eyes gleamed intently as he struck a match and moved it around the rim. They counted down twice, then cheered as the flaming thing finally lifted upwards before veering off to one side.

'Hmm, almost as good as yours, darling.'

'I agree,' said Charlie. 'Close, but no cigarillo.'

'Imagine how your little one will like that in years to come,' said Bob. 'He'll watch open-mouthed. Or she. She'll be so gob-smacked.'

'He's getting broody,' said Charlie.

'I'd better make that coffee,' said Clare.

'So what goes on at the rugger club, Steve?'

'Oh, nothing much - apart from rugger, of course. And drinking.'

'And the singing of some very coarse songs, no doubt?'

'Well, yes. Not all of them coarse, though.'

'Just filthy,' said Clare from the coffee maker.

'Give us an example,' said Bob.

'Well, I'd better not. I might get carried away.'

'Coward!'

'We do Eskimo Nell, of course, the Good Ship Venus, Dinah, Dinah, Show Us Your Leg. But we sing songs like the Wild Rover too. That's not filthy. And *Always Look On the Bright Side of Life*.'

'Ah, one of my all time favourites,' said Charlie. 'Perhaps I could come and join you in the showers some time and we'll sing it together?'

'Well-'

'Change the subject,' trilled Clare.

'We'll laugh at death as we lather each other.'

'Charlie!'

'I've changed the subject, dear. We're talking about death now. That's why I love the song. I too hope to face the curtain with a bow.'

'The curtain?' said Bob. 'Oh - *that* curtain.'

114

'Yes, *that* curtain. And that's how I shall face it - when the time comes...'

And half-rising from his chair, he demonstrated rather unsteadily.

'I'm sure you will if you're still in one piece,' said Clare.

'And not too drunk,' said Steve.

'Will God interpret your falling over as a bow - that's the thing?' said Bob.

Charlie sank back heavily into his chair.

'You are all complete and utter bar stewards,' he said.

'Here,' said Clare, setting coffee mugs in front of them. 'Drink this or you might be facing the curtain sooner than you think.'

'Oh, we'll be fine,' said Charlie. 'As long as the fucking air bags work.'

Half an hour later, they left with their hosts waving them off. Clare stayed on the doorstep until she could hear the car engine no longer, then went back to the kitchen where Steve had started loading the dishwasher.

'Listening for the sound of collision?' he asked.

'Oh they'll be all right - they always are. Hey, you're not hoping that's going to happen, are you?'

'Of course not.'

Clare leaned against him and stroked his shoulder.

'You're not very comfortable with them, are you?'

'They're okay. Quite fun. Probably not people I'd mix with if I didn't know you.'

'I'm sure you wouldn't. They're sweet guys, though. And they love each other like we do.'

'Well, not quite like we do.'

'I'm talking about the emotional side of it, silly. Not the physical side, not the mechanics.'

Steve shrugged.

'They do seem very fond of each other.'

He started to run water into the sink to wash the large pans. Clare picked up the tea towel ready to dry them.

'I'm glad they're coming to the wedding.'

'Well, yes. The more the merrier...'

'I would have liked them to be witnesses, but it's not-'

'We've got enough witnesses.'

115

'Well, okay. I just thought maybe one of them could be a witness on behalf of both, but then - which one? I suspect the other would feel hurt.'

'Hmm. Maybe. You know, the irony is - I actually think Charlie could have been quite a good rugby player.'

Clare couldn't help herself.

'Darling, you're starting to sound like Johnny One Note. And what do you mean - *could have been*? Do you mean - he could have been a good rugby player if he wasn't gay?'

Steve looked puzzled again.

'Well, yes. They're not known for playing rugger, are they? I also -' He hesitated, leaning on the edge of the sink.

'What?'

Clare was aware how her voice had become a little bit colder and crisper.

'I also think we should be careful - and they almost hinted at it tonight - but I don't think we should let them get too...involved when the baby arrives. I mean I don't think we should ask them to baby sit, for example. Thinking ahead, that is.'

'Well it hadn't occurred to me, but why on earth not?'

'Well, I just wouldn't be happy about it...particularly if it's a boy.'

'But it might be a girl...' She shook herself. 'What am I talking about? It doesn't matter whether it's a girl or a boy. Do you seriously imagine that they would...do anything? They're my friends, you know.'

She turned away. The shutters to the side window were still open and her image glared back at her from the outer darkness, all stiff shoulders and arched eyebrows and black pained eyes as if there was another burden she was carrying besides the baby.

'Well it's not just that. It's - well, it sets the wrong example, doesn't it? Two men together...I've nothing against that as you know, but we don't want our children when they're young - '

'So you're saying it would be okay if *one* of them babysat?'

'Well, I don't know - '

'Or if the baby's a girl?'

'Look, don't be angry. I'm just concerned - we've got to care for and protect our child. We can't take risks. You read about these things...'

'We can't decide people are a risk because they happen to be gay.'

'I-'

'It would be okay if one of your rugby playing mates was baby

116

sitting, would it? Singing dirty lullabies to it?'

'No! Of course not.'

Steve looked in exasperation at the ceiling, then lifted his arms out of the suds and turned to face her. But it was too late. The tea towel hit his chest.

'Here, you finish the job. I'm going to sit down. I've been on my feet most of the evening in case you haven't noticed.'

'Clare!'

His voice echoed along the hallway. The smell of that once delicious curry hung there too, stale and oppressive. She swung the living room door shut behind her and walked across to the walnut-framed mirror that hung over the fireplace. There was her normal face - a neatly trimmed black fringe, blue eyes, a sharp angular nose, a bow-shaped mouth with a little dimple underneath... She studied it for a moment or two but then was assailed by other thoughts - wild thoughts. She turned away, sat down on the sofa and automatically rested her hand on the bump. Almost as if in response, the baby kicked. She breathed slowly and deeply and let a tear roll halfway down her cheek before wiping it away. What could she do? Her course was set.

The door was pushed gently open and Steve stood there gazing down at her.

'Darling...' he said. 'I didn't mean to upset you. Is everything okay?'

'It's probably just the hormones,' she said without looking at him.

'Yes,' he said, nodding. 'I expect you're right. Is there anything I can do?'

'No,' she said, shaking her head. 'There's nothing.'

The Last Days of Dad

He hadn't been at work very long that day when the phone rang. It was the double ring of an outside call which usually meant 'personal' in his job. He picked up the receiver and said 'Hello' in a soft, cautious voice unlike his normal phone manner. Pattie's voice at the other end was also soft, but for a few seconds it filled his head.

'Will, I'm sorry. The rest home just rang.'

She paused and he knew what was coming.

'Yes?'

It came.

'Your father died this morning'.

'Oh no...'

Pattie paused again, then said:

'They checked on him during the night because obviously he wasn't very well. But this morning they couldn't wake him although he was still breathing. They called a doctor but it was too late. He died just before 9.00 am.'

'So that woman was right...'

'That woman was right...'

'How weird.'

'Yep.'

'I'll have to come home...'

'Okay.'

'We'll have to go up there.'

'We were going up there anyway next weekend...'

'I'll have to sort everything out.'

'*We'll* have to sort everything out. Your aunt and uncle will help. Geoff and Sue will put us up.'

'Okay. I'd better go and see the boss.'

'Let me know...'

'Speak to you soon.'

He put the receiver down and sat back in his chair. Time seemed to have paused as if waiting for his soul to respond and his soul wasn't quite ready. *Died. Your father has died. Your father...* The words echoed in his head. What did he feel? Relief? Disbelief? Strangeness? Nothing? What *should* he be feeling? Sorrow, surely. And a sense that

119

something momentous had occurred. *Just before 9.00 am.* What had he been doing? Coming out of the tube station, five minutes walk away. What *should* he be doing? He needed to tell other people at work and ask for time off again. Then drive north with his wife and baby son and talk to more people: the relatives and friends, the solicitor, the doctor, the funeral director, the registrar of birth, marriage and... I am at a loss, he thought. I have arrived at a loss.

He stood up and moved around the desk, hands in pockets, uncertain, brooding. He wasn't used to having an office of his own, to being alone within four walls. It felt isolating and uncomfortable. He knew that it had nothing to do with status or importance. He was a backroom boy now, doing "research" and could sit anywhere as long as he had a desk and computer. He had been moved into this room to stop it being snatched by Central Services. A blocking move. Every morning he had to get the key from Charity and return it to her or Tara at the end of the day. There were only a few things here that could be described as "his": a parlour palm on top of one of the filing cabinets, an old exhibition poster on the wall, a pile of paperwork on the desk and some files in the drawer. The locked cabinets, the skip full of old periodicals and microfilms, the bookcase containing directories and manuals were nothing to do with him.

He went across to the window and looked out. Over the wall, he could see the back gardens of a row of small hotels that would once have been large town houses. Now the gardens provided a strip of greenery, a soothing connection to the natural world and the passing seasons. Spring - it was mid-spring, warm and sunny; all things were growing and opening up. He watched sparrows flitting between the trees, probably nesting nearby. This was no time to give up on life, yet his mother had died in spring and now his father. And everything seemed to be in transition. He had a new job that he didn't properly understand with new rules that had to be followed as if the logic was obvious. He had a baby boy and life at home was changing too. Pattie wanted them to look for a new house which meant more stress, more pressure. He'd like a new house too but with a back garden like one of these before him with stout brick walls and borders of thick green bushes and trees where you wouldn't be overlooked in summer and could go and lie down on the grass and stare at those little white clouds drifting without haste across an endless blue sky. Supine meditation, relaxing every tense muscle, feeling the earth supporting your body, nothing to do but breathe and reflect. That would suffice for now.

He turned away and went to see his boss at the end of the corridor. Charity who sat in the outer office said that he could just go straight in. The door was ajar but he knocked before putting his head round it.

'Hi,' said Tara glancing up and then back to a document on the desk before her. She had her finger in the margin and was moving it down line by line as she absorbed the information. Will had had female bosses before, but this was the first time he had been managed by someone who wore bright red nail varnish and ornate rings. He took a few steps forward.

'I've just had some bad news, I'm afraid.'

'Oh.' She looked up again instantly concerned. 'Do sit down.'

He sat opposite her.

'Well it was kind of expected, but my wife just rang to say that my father died this morning.' He hoped that he'd got just the right level of emotion in his voice.

'Oh, I am sorry, Will. Had he been ill for long?'

'Well the illness was sudden but he'd been in decline since my mother died four years ago.'

'Oh, I see. He missed her a lot, I expect?'

'Yes. He missed her emotionally, but also in a practical sense. He wasn't used to fending for himself.'

Tara nodded.

'Yes, I can imagine.'

'Erm...' He sighed. 'I'm not sure...'

'I think you should probably go home, Will.'

'But I've only just got back from paternity leave...'

Tara looked briefly as if she'd forgotten that, but carried on nevertheless, looking directly at him with earnest brown eyes.

'Will, I want to feel that I'm leading a team of human beings. Your father dies and you carry on preparing budget figures and project milestones as if nothing had happened? I don't think so. I've got a good idea of where we are and we'll cope.'

'OK. Thanks Tara. I appreciate it. I was going to say - I'm the only child so a lot of things will fall on me to sort out'.'

'Well there you are then,' said Tara as if that proved her right. 'Go and do what you have to do and don't worry about work. Just ring me or

121

Charity next week and let us know when you think you'll be back. We'll sort out some compassionate leave for you.'

He got up to leave. At the door, he turned to thank her again and couldn't help noticing that the moving finger was already back in the margin of the document. But it was nice of her all the same. Indeed, one might almost say...compassionate.

When he got home, Luke had just fallen asleep after a bottle feed and Pattie was about to take him up to the cot in their bedroom. They stood in a shaft of sunlight in the hallway and she tilted Luke back in her arms so that Will could see his face. He kissed both of them and Pattie stroked his shoulder and whispered '*I'm sorry.*' After she had gone upstairs, he took his jacket and tie off and made a pot of tea. When she came back, they hugged and then sat down at the kitchen table.

'So what did they say at work?'

'Oh, they were fine. Full of sympathy, condolences, etcetera. I told Charity but I think she'd already guessed - or maybe she'd overheard my conversation with Tara. I told Brian and he said in a rather anguished way "I'm sorry, I don't know what to say". I ended up almost consoling him, but at least he was genuine.'

'And what's Tara said about time off?'

'No problem. Just go and do what you've got to do. She gave me a brief lecture about wanting her staff to be human beings, i.e. people who have normal feelings and emotions, then went back to the document she was reading.'

'She's an alien leading a team of humans, trying to fit in.'

'I'm never sure about her. I suppose it's part of her professionalism that you don't know whether she's genuinely nice or heartless underneath.'

'She's somewhere in between, I expect. Anyway, how are you?'

She put her hand over his.

'I'm okay. I don't really feel anything very much, to be honest. Not so far. Just a bit stressed about everything I've got to do.'

'It seems a bit unreal to me - that woman rings your auntie last night and says "he's willing himself to die" - and then the next morning he dies...'

'Yes I still haven't taken it in.'

'I suppose it was - not easier, that's the wrong word - it had more direct impact when your mother died.'

'Well that was totally out of the blue. And he rang me himself. I had to cope with his grief as well as my own feelings.'

'I came with you to Euston, didn't I? We'd only been together a few months. I was in tears when you left.'

'Do you remember when we were standing on the tube platform and that empty train passed through? With all the carriages in darkness...'

'Vaguely. I didn't think about it till you said something....'

'It carried on like that. Did I tell you?'

'Sort of...'

'I missed the connection at Preston and had to wait an hour on this almost deserted platform. It was Sunday. The station buffet was closed for redecoration or something. The indicator boards were all blank, the announcers voice sounded like it came out of a vault...'

Pattie couldn't help smiling.

'It was like that song - "*I asked my captain for the time of day/He said he throwed his watch away*".'

'Well it won't be like that this time. We've got the car.'

'True. And little Luke to worry about.'

'Shall I ring Sue and see if we can stay with them for a few days? It's only three months before their baby is due.'

'Yes please. After that, I'd better ring Auntie Flo and then the funeral director.'

'Is it going to be the same man who buried your mother?'

'I suppose so. Mr Tulk. The incredible Tulk. He buried Uncle George as well. And Aunty Beth before him. He seems to have the concession.'

While Pattie used the phone, he wandered into the living room and sat down in 'his' armchair. There was a coffee table alongside with a few books on it and yesterday's paper folded open at the crossword. The previous evening's call from Auntie Flo played through his head again. It had been 9.25, less than 12 hours before his father had died. Neither his aunt nor his uncle had ever rung him before. The conversation had been halting and strained. He'd had to keep repeating his questions or wait while she repeated them back to him.

'Did we know he had flu, did you say?'

'Yes.'

'No. No-one told us a thing.'

Pause.

'When did you last see him?'

123

'When did we last him?'

'Yes.'

'It was a couple of weeks ago we went to see him. He didn't say much.'

They had never really liked their brother-in-law. He was polite enough, but there was something about him, something slightly different. He thought himself superior - or so they believed. He expressed his opinions with a knowing certainty and if anyone said anything otherwise, he didn't respond but just sniffed. He offered the bare minimum of small talk. Since their sister had died, he had become quite morose and even more uncommunicative - which was only natural, they supposed - but it was a struggle to help him.

'What did this woman say?'

'She said she used to be a neighbour of your mum and dad's at Woodvale Road.'

'I remember her.'

'You know. After they left the old house and before they moved to the bungalow.'

'Yes.'

'She said she was sorry for disturbing us...'

'Yep.'

'...but your father was willing himself to die.'

'*Willing himself to die?*'

'What? Yes. *Willing himself to die.* That's what she said. She sounded quite upset about it.'

'Why did she think that?'

'Why? Well, she said he wasn't very well but was refusing to take his medicine. Or he'd let it dribble out of the corner of his mouth while they weren't looking. And hide his pills.'

'And this woman works there? I didn't know that.'

'What did you say? I think she just started there recently. She said she remembered his name - that's right - when the other nurses talked about him, but when she saw him, she hardly recognised him.'

'Oh, dear.'

'In any case, he'd turned on his side facing the wall...not talking to anybody.'

He had talked to Pattie about it afterwards. How could you "will yourself to die"? The woman was being over-dramatic. They were looking after him in the rest home and he would get better again whether he liked it or not...

Pattie came into the living room.

'That's fine. It's all fixed up. Sue sends her love and sympathy.'

He took the phone from her, found his aunt's stored number and pressed the button.

That night, he took the first turn when Luke started crying. Lifting the baby out of the cot, he talked softly in his ear as he carried him downstairs. Surely his father had never done this with him? Wasn't it always the mother's job in those days? So many questions he'd never asked them. He warmed the bottle of baby milk in the microwave, shook it and ran it under cold water, tested it on the back of his hand, then went into the living room and sat on the sofa for a change. He switched on the television and watched a few minutes of some old American film. Meanwhile, a tiny pair of pink lips sucked on the teat and a tiny pair of blue eyes regarded him solemnly. Luke drank most of the milk but eventually pulled his mouth away. Will stood up and, holding the baby against his shoulder, paced back and forward across the living room, patting his back every now and again to try and wind him. After a few minutes of this, Luke finally gave a loud burp. Will looked down at him with a great beaming smile and kissed him on the brow.

'Gotcha,' he said and a minute later his son's eyes started to close.

He lay in bed again in the dark. The wind was blowing through the new leaves on the old pear tree in the garden. When it paused, he could hear his wife's regular breathing from the pillow next to him. He closed his eyes. His father was waiting in his faded pyjamas, gaunt and white haired, stubble glistening with medicine. He'd had enough, he wanted to die. He had wanted to die since that morning four years ago when he'd been unable to wake his wife. But his misery seemed to go back before then. Twenty or more years ago on one of their Sunday walks down on the front, they'd talked about average life spans. "I'll only have about five more years" he'd said. But apart from haemorrhoids, there had never really been anything wrong with him. And instead of dying, he had just got older, set in his narrow ways, maximising every affliction. "I never thought I'd outlive your mum" he'd said after the funeral. Her death was sudden and unexpected and he'd never given a thought to the fact that she might go before him. For a while, he had looked after himself, heating up tinned or frozen food, doing basic cleaning, going out once or twice a week to prowl around the library or the supermarket. It seemed to work. Will's aunt and uncle had "kept an eye on him" but he didn't crave company other than his wife's. He had even been to the church in the little town centre - as he'd told Will in one of his rare letters - to say a prayer and talk to her, even though he wasn't a believer. Then the phone had rung with the news that he'd had a stroke. A minor stroke but it had left him diminished, a little less able physically, a little less inclined mentally to look after himself. Will had driven up and stayed with him for a few days. He had shopped for him, cooked a few simple meals for him, cleaned out the kitchen which was filthy. He had slept in his old bedroom next to his father's and heard him crying in the night. Not just shedding tears but crying out aloud for his wife - this man who had been so reticent and self-contained - calling the name of his partner for 42 years. And there was nowhere Will could go and nothing he could do, but lie there on the edge of the nightmare and listen to the desolate wailing.

In time the social services arrived on the scene. A nurse began calling once a week, as did a cleaner. His aunt or uncle shopped for him once a week. Will phoned every Sunday, usually with a pre-dinner gin and tonic at his side to give him strength. A social worker called James was assigned to 'the case' and started ringing Will to suggest various options. Will drove up again for a face to face discussion. James had pink cheeks and looked as if he had only recently left school. His hair stuck up, his tie was askew and he blinked earnestly behind black-framed spectacles. They had sat in the living room with his father.

'We're here to support you, Mr Faraday,' said James. 'But it is important that you try to help yourself too and stay active and socially involved. Now there's a day centre you could go to - not necessarily every day, but maybe two or three times a week. You'd be picked up and taken there and back and you'd get a mid-day meal and they organise various activities...'

His father grunted and looked away.

'Or there's the option of moving into residential accommodation where there'd be a warden on site to provide any emergency assistance and a communal area where you could mix with other residents...'

'I don't want that,' said his father.

126

'Well what would you like to do then, Mr Faraday? The thing is, you're going to find it harder and harder to look after yourself here, even with the support you're getting.'

There was a pause and then, without looking at Will, his father had said:

'I want to go and live with my son.'

Will had tried to conceal both his panic and his antipathy. They had never talked about that and it came as a surprise, but perhaps was half-expected or half-feared.

'You know that wouldn't work, Dad. You wouldn't like living in the big city. It would be very different to what you're used to. And we both work during the day so there'd be nobody there to look after you. And you know that we're trying to start a family. If Pattie gets pregnant, it would be a lot for us to cope with.'

He knew he was talking as much to James as to his father.

'The other alternative,' said James after blinking carefully at both of them 'would be for you to move into a rest home...'

A rest home, a rest...and then he and his father were walking along the front again but with Pattie instead of his mother, lugging suitcases, struggling in a gale that drove sea spray into the air and over the railings almost to their feet. And Pattie kept one hand on her belly which was now expanded with child. And his father was more like his younger opinionated self, leading them onwards until the sun came out and they entered the calm of a side street and stopped before a large red-bricked house that looked like a boarding house. Here they were ushered through a conservatory by the silver haired manageress who called it "our sun lounge" and then talked about money while old ladies frowned at them from wing-backed armchairs. On they went through narrow carpeted corridors to the room booked for his father. And there was all sorts of confusion and James and his aunt and uncle were standing outside and his father was sitting on the bed crying for his wife again and saying - 'I don't want to live here, I don't want to live' - but the manageress just took Will and Pattie along the corridor and showed them the next room where they could stay 'at least until you have the baby, dear' and saying 'he'll have settled in by then'.

And then he was awake again momentarily with Pattie lying beside him and the wind still rustling the leaves of the pear tree bearing him back to sleep.

They set off in their little blue car on Sunday morning. Luke was strapped into his infant car seat in the back and Pattie sat next to him. The sun blind was in place and the Baby On Board sticker adorned the rear window. Welcomed by signs and cameras, they cruised through the Blackwall Tunnel and along the East London highways, after which it was just one damn motorway after another. Will drove cautiously at first, rarely venturing out of the inside lane. Later, bored and impatient, he used whichever lane let him reach the speed limit. They stopped twice to feed and change Luke and to grab snacks and coffees. Finally, they rolled into Geoff and Sue's driveway just as the sun was starting its glowing descent over the sea. There was no sign of life at the front of the house, so they had time to unstrap Luke and arrange themselves on the doorstep as a little family unit before ringing the bell.

Sue gave Will a sympathy hug first and he felt the hard yet vulnerable curves of her belly. Then she threw her arms around Pattie and cooed over Luke.

'You'll have to be Auntie Sue now,' said Pattie.

Geoff shook Will's hand and offered manly condolences.

'So this is the little chap,' he said.

'This is him.'

'Very nice. Couldn't have done better myself.'

'Well, we'll soon find out,' said Will.

They went through the hallway into the big kitchen where the women sat and the men stood as they toasted the baby with cava.

'I'm only having a sip,' said Sue. 'I envy you now, Pattie.'

They talked about pregnancies and babies and sleepless nights. Then Will hauled the main items of luggage out of the car and he and Pattie went up to their allotted bedroom to unpack and set up the travel cot.

When they came down, the dining table in the back room had been set with placemats and best cutlery and rolled cloth napkins. The men had red wine, Pattie had white and Sue had some kind of flavoured water. They sat - with clinking of glasses - to a starter of avocado stuffed with crabmeat.

'You're doing us proud here,' said Will.

'Well it's a big occasion,' said Sue.

'In more ways than one,' said Geoff. His voice was deep and calm.

'Yes, are they any clearer about the cause of your dad's death, Will?'

Will shrugged.

'I'm collecting the death certificate from the doctor's tomorrow. I don't think there's any mystery about it. He had flu and just didn't want to fight it.'

'Well, at that age...And didn't he have a stroke not long ago?'

Will told them the story of the woman who'd said he was "willing himself to die".

'Hmm...he hadn't been very happy since your mother died, had he?'

'That's an understatement. He couldn't see any reason to carry on living.'

'Not even when he knew he had a grandson?'

'Well, that's a peculiar thing. I've thought about that. We sent him some photos and told him Luke's name and so on. My mother died without seeing any grandchildren. At least he knew that the family line was being carried on and maybe that was enough for him.'

'But wouldn't he at least want to see his grandson and hold him?'

'Yes.' said Will 'but...' This was getting too personal. And he hadn't thought about it before, but it would have been beautiful if his father had held Luke, even just one time for the photograph album.

'Who knows? I could speculate for ever. He was always very set in his ways and I think playing the role of a grandad was beyond him. He'd had enough. And when he fell ill, he just went with it. From what that woman said, he made a deliberate effort to avoid taking medicine.'

'I still don't see how you can make yourself die, though. He must have been in a weaker condition than anybody realised.'

'Maybe,' said Will. 'I just don't know. He was a closed book. He never really told me what he felt or thought.'

'Basically, you were estranged, weren't you?' said Pattie.

'I wouldn't say that. We were miles apart, but there was still some sort of connection. He did actually write me a few letters in which he partly expressed his feelings, but in person, he couldn't open up. He would make these pronouncements, but couldn't or wouldn't discuss them. I knew if I argued with anything he said, he'd get annoyed or resentful. And that made me uncomfortable.'

Sue nodded and said 'Hmm' but no-one else spoke. Will carried on to fill the silence.

'Even in those letters, he expressed himself in cliches, trite sentiments. He was quite self-pitying really, quite maudlin.'

'Quite what?' said Geoff.

'Maudlin. It means...self-pitying, tearful...cloyingly sentimental.'

129

'You know, one day Luke might sit in judgement on you,' said Pattie with a glance at the infant who was sleeping in his basket on the sofa.

'I never had a go at my dad - not after I left home anyway. I just put up with him. And he won't be hurt by anything I say about him now.'

'That's for sure,' said Geoff. 'Here, have another glass. There's no point worrying about all that now. What will be will be - Will!'

Sue laughed and said:

'I bet you're looking forward to the will, Will!'

He was grateful for the lightening of mood. While the starter plates were cleared away and lasagne and salad was produced for the main course, he thought of a story to tell them although Pattie knew it already.

'Did I ever tell you about the little box he gave me?'

'Little box? - no...'

'He gave it to me a couple of years ago when I was staying with him for a few days. He'd been sorting through some of the stuff in their bedroom and he came shuffling into my room with this little box in his hand and said "this'll be more use to you now than me". I opened it and - what do you think it contained?'

'A ring of your mum's?' said Sue.

'A pair of false teeth,' said Geoff.

'Contraceptives,' said Will.

'Oh my God'.

'I said "Actually dad, we're thinking of starting a family". He laughed. We both laughed. I suppose it brought us together for a moment. But it struck me afterwards that it was almost like a rite of passage - the father handing something on to the son, you know, to mark his entry into adulthood.'

'Except twenty years too late,' said Pattie.

'Well, almost. Anyway, I thought these things looked a bit old-fashioned - they were quite plain and thick. So after he'd gone out of the room I looked on the underside of the box. The Use By date had expired sixteen years earlier.'

'Oh my God. That says something doesn't it?'

'It says they should have tried the extra ribbed, strawberry flavoured ones.'

'Geoff. Behave. These are Will's parents we're talking about.'

'Exactly,' said Will. 'It's hard to imagine them - well, obviously they did, otherwise I wouldn't be here. But I don't think they were really into the physical side of it. Anyway I thought he might be coming out of it at that point, you know. Getting over it, throwing stuff in the bin, finding something to laugh about. But then a few weeks later, he had the stroke and that was the beginning of the end.'

'You had to put him in a rest home eventually, didn't you?' said Sue.

'Well, yes - to cut a long story short.'

'Didn't he run away from it at one point?'

'Yes, that was the first rest home. We thought it was working out okay, didn't we?'

'Well, he wasn't very happy that time we visited him, but then he was never very happy,' said Pattie.

'He never expressed any desire to leave. He never said anything more about moving in with us as he had done before. Then one morning I got a phone call at work from James, the boy wonder social worker who was on our case. "Your father's gone missing. Walked out of the rest home." He was going to call the police, but I rang home and my dad answered. He'd just packed a suitcase, sneaked out when no-one was looking and got on the bus back home. I was quite impressed in a way. Seventy five years old and he'd gone AWOL. I said to him: "Do you remember when I ran away from home when I was a little boy". He went quiet. I think he might have been -'

'You ran away from home?'

'Well, sort of. But that's another story. Anyway, I came up again to defend him from James. In the end, he agreed to go to this day centre twice a week. He got the cleaner back that he'd had before, my aunt and uncle helped out, I came up once a fortnight throughout the autumn. Then...well, you know what happened when we came up at the end of January.'

'He looked like Ben Gunn, Pattie said'.

'He'd grown a beard. He was very thin,' said Pattie.

'Well, I didn't want to talk about it too much while we were staying with you but I was shocked. I hadn't seen him since before Christmas. He'd sounded normal when I spoke to him on the phone and I just assumed everything was okay. I didn't realise he'd stopped going to the day centre. Why hadn't James been on the phone to me? He said he didn't know. Why hadn't my aunt and uncle told me? They said: "Well, we didn't want to worry you with Pattie expecting". I think they'd been round there and he wouldn't let them in the door.'

'And yet from what you said, his mind wasn't wandering or anything.'

'He was lucid when I talked to him, but when no-one was there I think he just retreated so far into his memories and into the past that he didn't care about the present.'

'I remember you showed him the ultrasound picture.'

'I had to say to him: look Dad, we can't cope with this any more. Nobody can cope with it. I need to concentrate on looking after Pattie and your future grandson. And I showed him the picture. I'm not sure whether he could really see the baby but he said "oh aye".'

'Oh aye.'

'That was when he agreed to go back into a rest home, though, wasn't it?' said Pattie. 'I think seeing me so pregnant brought it home.'

'Yeah, he could hardly come back with the old 'I just want to die' schtick,' said Will.

'Wh-what?' said Geoff.

'Schtick. Jewish word meaning routine or repeated performance.'

'You can tell he's a librarian, can't you?'

'But they found him a nicer place,' said Sue. 'In the local area rather than on the other side of town.'

'Yeah...you know I nearly took his house keys when we were moving him in. He put them down somewhere and I slipped them into my pocket. But then I thought what if he goes back to the house and can't get in? I can't be his jailer. I gave them back to him and he said "Oh, I won't need those any more".'

And Will had gone back to the car and shed a few - just one or two - tears before driving away. But for now he looked down into his wine glass without saying anything further and the conversation moved on.

'How was it then, Pattie?' asked Sue. 'Tell us the gory details. Well, not too gory, obviously.'

In bed, Pattie said:

'Aren't you going to see him in the mortuary?'

'It's called the Chapel of Rest,' Will said slowly and thickly while the bedroom walls advanced and the blood shrilled in his ears.

'Well, you told me you went to see your mum...I just wondered.'

Will tried to think.

'I went to see my mother...it was so unexpected...I took my dad. He was hopeless. He lasted less than half a minute, then went out and sat down and cried. The lady on reception gave him a tissue. That made him embarrassed...'

132

'Aw...I expect they keep a big supply of tissues.'

'She wasn't in the coffin - they'd laid her out in her own clothes on a sort of...I don't know...soft table...with a little pillow under her head. She looked quite normal as if she could wake up any moment. It took me back to when I was a kid and I visited her in hospital...and she dozed off and I got anxious.'

The moment shimmered in his mind again. Was she going to wake up? Was he dreaming?

'I wouldn't go if it were me,' he heard Pattie say.

'I'm not going. There's no point. He's dead. He's *gone*...'

'What's the point?'

'The point is...to pay your respects...and say goodbye. But there's no point.'

'You can do that at the funeral'.

He yawned again and wondered vaguely if she'd been listening or if he'd been talking to himself. And then before he knew where he was...he was unconscious.

Next day, up late and with a medium-sized hangover, Will did the rounds. He went first to the doctor's to get the medical death certificate, then walked a few hundred yards through the streets of suburbia to his aunt and uncle's house on the main road. From there, his uncle drove him to the District Register Office where the details of his father's death were recorded with soft-toned sympathy by a female clerk. After that, they drove to the other aunt and uncle's house for a ham roll lunch and then back to the little town centre to drop off a copy of the death certificate at the solicitor's and make an appointment for the reading of the will. Finally, they called at the rest home - a large old red brick Victorian house which had an overgrown garden at the front but was all spick and span inside. A bubble-haired blonde woman fetched a suitcase on wheels and a large cloth bag which contained all the possessions his father had brought there. After glancing around as if to see whether anyone was listening, she asked:

'Would you like to see the room that your father passed away in?'

He followed her glance towards the dark mahogany staircase that led to the upper realms where somewhere out of sight his father's life had ended. It was an unexpected question and he made a snap decision.

'No, it's all right, thanks.'

On the Tuesday morning, they went to see the vicar. Pattie carried Luke in a sling against her bosom and Will had the changing bag over one shoulder.

'What do you think he'll say to all this?'

'Nothing,' said Will. 'I've met him before. He's too repressed. He copes with the modern world by not saying anything about it. It's a pity you're not breast-feeding, though. That would really put something in his pipe.'

'Is he a pipe smoker, then?'

'I speak metaphorically, dear.'

'I know. Just joking.'

'If you were breast feeding, he'd probably send you out of the room. Ask his wife to find some cubby hole that you could sit in.'

'A broom cupboard.'

'She'd probably shoo you out of the house with a broom.'

'The garden shed?'

'Still too close. She'd drive you out of the parish altogether. I'd have to come and look for you in some barn...'

The vicar's wife had given him directions over the phone the previous day. Before reaching the churchyard, they turned off the high street into a cobbled cul-de-sac lined with dainty little shops. The vicarage stood at the end. It was a modern affair with a flat roof and frosted glass front door and clashed somewhat with its olde-worlde surroundings. The vicar himself let them in. He was a couple of inches shorter than Will with a pointy nose, soured apple cheeks and once-golden hair that time had thinned and bleached. Will introduced himself, Pattie and the sleeping Luke and the vicar obliged with an uneasy smile before leading them into a book-lined study just off the hallway. Will scanned the nearest bookshelf as he sat down but every dull spine had a theological title. The vicar sat behind his desk. A notepad and fountain pen lay before him.

'First of all, my commiserations on the death of your father,' he said evenly. 'I'm afraid I didn't know him, but I'm sure he was a good man.'

'You didn't know him because he didn't go to church - yours or anyone else's. I should say at the outset that he wasn't a believer and neither am I.'

'I see. Well, that won't necessarily be a problem. These days I often conduct services for people who either profess not to be believers or who have left no indication of their beliefs.'

Will smiled. He felt relaxed and confident.

'Okay, well I don't "profess" to be a non-believer. I *am* a non-believer. As for my dad, I'm pretty sure from things he said during his life that he didn't believe either. Having said that, he did come into your church once to say a prayer, but I think he was just trying to make himself feel better.'

'Why do you think he needed to make himself feel better?'

Will shrugged.

'My mother died suddenly, unexpectedly. There was no big deathbed scene, no opportunity for him to talk to her and tell her things and hold her hand.'

'I see. Tell me a few details about him.'

'He loved my mother - I think that's the main fact. They got married after only a few months of courtship and were together for forty-two years. There was never any real tension in their relationship. They stayed true to their wedding vows, I suppose you could say. Apart from that, he was a big science-fiction fan at one time and had a collection of books and magazines that took up a whole room. He retired a few years early because of ill-health and didn't really do much after that. Watched TV, read detective novels, pottered about, did a bit of gardening. He led a quiet life really.'

The vicar had been scribbling notes and looked up when Will paused.

'It's interesting that the first thing that came to your mind was how much he loved your mother. That connects him with the love that's at the heart of the Christian faith. The divine love that God shows by His willingness to forgive.'

Will was amazed at this tortuous nonsense. And angry. He hadn't come here to be preached at. Was this guy never out of the pulpit? But he stayed calm.

'God doesn't exist. And I don't think my parents needed to be forgiven for anything. Theirs was just normal human love - like ours.' And he gestured towards Pattie and Luke. 'A miracle if you like - I mean the fact that we exist at all is a miracle - but nothing to do with some supreme being. I mean, when you look at all the suffering and misery that humans undergo, the idea of divine love is just a joke.'

The vicar spoke in a quieter voice than before.

'I see. I was referring to the divine love that gives eternal life, but let's press on. What was your father's occupation?'

135

'He was just a clerk with an insurance company. He never wanted or sought any kind of career advance. He just wanted to do a good job. He was a very honest man. My mother used to call him "Honest Bill".'

The vicar put his pen down.

'Well, that's enough to be going on with.'

'To be going on with?'

'For the funeral service. It's customary for me to say a few words about the deceased - his character, his interests and so on.'

'Oh no,' said Will flatly. 'I don't want that sort of service and neither would my father. With all due respect, I don't want to listen to a speech by someone who never knew him. Or sit through hymns and prayers with everyone just muttering because they don't know the words or they're too embarrassed.'

The vicar looked grim.

'It would be quite in order for you to stand up and say a few words about your father if you prefer.'

Will felt tense.

'I just want him to be buried with my mother and for us to say our goodbyes in our own way at the graveside.'

'I see,' said the vicar. 'Well I can do a graveside ceremony but there has to be some sort of service.'

'What did you have in mind?'

The vicar picked up a black book from his desk, thumbed through it, moved the inbound bookmark to a particular page and passed it across the desk to Will.

'The basics are on that and the next few pages. I won't include all of it but it gives you an idea.'

Will glanced quickly through the pages.

'Do you have to say that?' He held up the book and pointed at the lines that begin *Man that is born of a woman...*

The vicar leant forward squinting.

'Well, yes. It's an integral part of the burial service.'

Will stopped himself from saying 'Jesus!'

'Well, as long as there's nothing that we have to chant out loud or repeat after you.'

'Won't there be any other relatives or friends coming along who might want to join in?'

'He had no friends. Not by the end of his life. There'll be a few relatives but they're not from his side of the family and they'll just have to respect my wishes. They weren't very fond of him in any case.'

'I see. You're quite sure that this is what your father would have wanted?'

'He would have wanted the minimum fuss, I'm sure of that. He would have just wanted to be put in the ground. No sentimental tosh spoken about him and as little religious ceremony as possible.'

'Very well.'

'I take it you have no objection to the baby being present? We can't leave him with anyone else.'

'I wouldn't normally encourage young children to attend funerals. I think it can be upsetting for them. But your baby won't be aware.'

'Suffer the little children,' said Will.

'Indeed, but don't make them suffer.'

'He'll probably sleep through it,' said Pattie.

'If that's all, I will see you at the cemetery on Friday.'

As they stood up, Will said:

'You have a lot of books, vicar. Have you got Joseph Conrad's Heart of Darkness by any chance?'

'I'm afraid not,' said the vicar who walked rapidly around his desk and held the study door open for them. He was clearly not going to rise to anything that might further insult his beliefs. He showed them out of the house in silence and responded only with a nod of the head when they said 'thank you' and 'goodbye'.

'Did you see that?' said Will after the door had closed. 'Not very Christian.'

'Well you weren't very nice,' said Pattie. 'Poor man - I was cringing in my seat.'

They walked down the short cobbled close. A faint sun was shining through the clouds.

'Oh he stood up for himself in his own way. It's just that I've seen too many of these funerals in the last few years. It's a conveyor belt system. Here's the next wooden box - bit of music, few words about his favourite football team, his hobbies, how his family loved him, obliging snivels from the front row, a few hymns that no-one really sings any more, depressing prayers...'

'Well what did you want? A New Orleans marching band?'

'I don't know. Just something that's somehow meaningful...or not too meaningless.'

'And what was that about Joseph Conrad?'

'Heart of Darkness, my dear. You should read it. After the great Kurtz dies in the jungle, Conrad writes: *Next day the pilgrims buried something in a muddy hole.* I was going to run that past him.'

'You're wicked. He's probably on his knees right now praying for help.'

'Well he'd better pick himself up again.'

On the Wednesday morning, they met Mr Tulk at his aunt and uncle's house to arrange the final details of the funeral. He and Pattie sat with Luke on the sofa while his aunt made a pot of tea. His uncle sat on a dining chair by the window half-facing the main road and peered through the slats of the Venetian blind from time to time as if he welcomed any distraction. Mr Tulk perched on the edge of the guest armchair. Sombre suited, his features, body language and voice spoke of a working lifetime of commiseration and diplomacy, of attempting to smooth the rough edges of pain.

'It will be a horse drawn carriage, won't it?' Will asked. "Black horses, of course.'

Mr Tulk permitted himself a brief smile.

'I'm afraid not, Mr Faraday.'

'No mutes?'

'Alas, the funeral plan doesn't allow for any mutes, heh heh.'

'What are mutes?' asked Pattie.

Will explained.

'They don't exist any more, do they Mr Tulk?'

'Long gone, Mr Faraday.'

'Dead and buried, you might say. Mute for ever.'

Mr Tulk compressed his lips as if it wouldn't do to smile this time. Will wondered if he ever laughed out loud or danced a little jig or even whistled. What was Christmas like in his house? Had he turned somersaults as a child or raced to the end of the street? He looked at his uncle, but his uncle just shook his head as if he disapproved of the whole conversation.

Will explained to Mr Tulk what had been agreed with the vicar. They discussed the arrangements and went out to the car so Will could show

how the baby seat worked. Mr Tulk agreed to turn up five minutes earlier than planned in case there was any difficulty.

'Of course, I'm sure no-one ever crashes into a funeral car,' said Will.

'Not as a rule, Mr Faraday, but we do have to comply with the law. And make sure your son is safe, of course.'

'And what if Luke starts crying during the service?' asked his aunt when they were back inside.

'I'll just walk him up and down,' said Pattie. 'We'll be outside, don't forget.'

'Honestly, the older generation,' said Will later as they waved goodbye. 'All they ever do is worry.'

They drove the short distance to his parents' bungalow and spent a couple of hours sorting through his father's possessions. Will had brought a cardboard box into which he placed the remnants of his father's library to take back home. Some HG Wells and Conan Doyle, Stoker's Dracula, some sci-fi, some classic crime story anthologies and the orange paperback edition of Lady Chatterley's Lover. They made a small pile of ornaments and the like which his relatives might be interested in. Everything else would go during the house clearance.

They ate lunch at a cafe in the little town centre. A friendly woman behind the counter warmed Luke's bottle of milk in the microwave. Then it was on to the solicitors where Will was given a copy of the will to read. There were no surprises. Everything had been left to him - a few thousand pounds in savings, some shares in privatised utility companies and the bungalow which would be sold. He tried not to look pleased.

It rained during the night but on the morning of the funeral, the sun came out and there was a fresh breeze blowing from the sea. Will hadn't brought a suit, but he dressed in dark grey trousers, white shirt, black tie and a soft black jerkin.

'That looks sombre enough, doesn't it?' he said to Pattie.

'Where's the balaclava?'

'What?'

'You look like an IRA gunman.'

Will laughed.

'I don't want to frighten Luke at such an early age.'

'Actually, you look quite attractive...'

They arrived at his aunt and uncle's house at 10.30. The other aunt and uncle were there too, dressed in their Sunday best. At 10.40 prompt, the hearse and a black Daimler drew up on the road outside. As they walked down the driveway, they saw the coffin with its gleaming brass handles and, on its lid, two wreaths from the relatives and a spray of white roses that he and Pattie had ordered. Will opened the back door of the Daimler and as he had expected the child seat could only be half-fixed around the seat. Nevertheless, Luke was strapped into it and Pattie sat next to him holding it down while Mr Tulk seemed not to notice, his eyes flitting elsewhere. The aunts and uncles got into his uncle's car, the hearse pulled away and they set off along the road behind it at a stately 20 mph.

'When we get there, the hearse will stop just inside the entrance, then the coffin will be taken straight to the graveside in accordance with your wishes,' said Mr Tulk comfortingly.

'Thank you.'

'We'll park by the chapel and then walk back to the graveside.'

'Fine.'

Apart from pleasantries about the weather, nothing further was said as the car moved quietly and smoothly along the road. Will calculated that this was the fifth time he had made this journey after his mother's funeral and those of three relatives who were buried in the same cemetery. As they drew closer, he recognised the familiar landmarks. A small industrial estate, a row of high bungalows with terraced front gardens and then the long row of poplar trees which screened the cemetery from the road. At the far end of this row, the oncoming traffic stopped and let them turn slowly to the right and in between the cemetery gates. The hearse pulled over to one side while the Daimler continued along a straight tarmac path. On either side were graves topped with weather-beaten monuments: ordinary crosses and Celtic crosses, urns and open books set in stone, winged angels in pious poses. Then they came to the little brick and wood chapel which had a small parking area alongside it. They got out of the car and Mr Tulk and his driver helped the aunts and uncles out of their car. After a minute or two, the vicar emerged from the chapel in his white robe holding the black book in his hands. He greeted them with a single 'good morning', gestured with his hand back along the path and then led them to the graveside. The coffin was on a metal stand and long brown straps had been wrapped under it and up through the handles.

The wreaths and spray lay to one side. The name and dates of Will's mother were engraved on the headstone and the spot was close to the road. Will remembered that his father had been pleased because there was open space and a bench a few feet away where he could sit on his visits. He hadn't been there since his stroke and nor had Will. The bench had gone and a row of new headstones extended almost to the edge of the path.

The vicar took his place at the foot of the open grave. The mourners stood on the grass along one side and Will imagined what they must look like from a distance - a motley ragged line of young and old. The youngest was dressed all in white under a floppy cotton hat. Will took hold of him carefully from Pattie and kissed him lightly on the cheek. For a moment, they looked at each other and then Luke's eyes switched to something else. Will felt glad that his son was awake and tried to hold him so that both were facing forward. He was not above the notion that somehow his mother and father might be watching as if through some anomaly in time. The vicar began:

I am the resurrection and the life, saith the Lord...

Cars went by on the road, birds continued to sing and the top leaves of the poplars swayed in the breeze. The vicar droned on and Will stood slowly rocking his son as the minutes ticked silently by. He knew that this day would one day dawn for him, or rather would not dawn for him but for those who came after.

Man that is born of a woman hath but a short time to live and is full of misery...

The undertakers' men began to lower the coffin:

We therefore commit his body to the ground: earth to earth, ashes to ashes, dust to dust...

There was a tray of soil at their feet and when the coffin had settled into its hole, the vicar invited them to throw a handful after it. Will went first and said 'Goodbye Dad' loud enough - he hoped - to be heard. Then he moved aside to let the others take their turn. What did it all mean? The answer still eluded him. He looked at his watch. The whole ceremony had taken 12 minutes. He walked around to look at the card on the spray of white flowers. The florist who had written the message in blue biro after he had dictated it over the phone had got it right. It read: 'In loving memory of a father, father-in-law and grandfather from Will, Pattie and grandson Luke.' Those last two words...He took a deep breath to control the sudden swell of emotion and hugged the quiet little bundle he was holding against his chest. 'Good boy' he said. 'Good boy. Good grandson.'

The vicar was waiting on the path as they left the graveside. Will thanked him and feeling the need to add something said:

'That was just right.'

'Good,' said the vicar. 'It's a fine morning. Perhaps it wasn't such a bad idea after all to hold it in the open air.'

'You should do it more often.'

They joined the main path that led back to the chapel and the car park.

'You know something you said to me the other day has stayed in my mind,' said the vicar.

'Oh yes?'

'You said that your father had gone into a church and prayed even though he wasn't a believer. Is that right?'

'Well, he went into *your* church. I don't know if it was deliberate or just a spur of the moment thing as he was passing by.'

'It doesn't matter,' said the vicar with a note of mild exasperation in his voice. 'He went into a church which is the house of God on earth and said a prayer which is a way of communing with God.'

Will sighed. He felt mildly exasperated too.

'I may have said that he prayed, but I think he was just trying to commune with my mother really - from what I remember of his letter.'

'All I want to say to you is that God will have heard him. God will have heard his prayer.'

'Really?' Will couldn't help himself. 'He's an amazing guy, isn't he?'

The vicar looked down at the ground for a few seconds as if it helped to watch his legs moving purposefully forward.

'God's powers are beyond our comprehension,' he said.

'They're certainly beyond mine.'

Pattie had caught up with them and overheard the last few exchanges.

'Shall we get into the car?' she said.

He nodded.

'Thanks again. I do appreciate it.'

The vicar inclined his head in a farewell gesture but said no more and walked away towards the chapel.

'Honestly, Will... He was just trying to make you feel a bit better.'

They spent that night at the bungalow intending to tidy and clean the next morning before an estate agent arrived to value the property. Will had discovered that the living room sofa could be opened out into a bed and they found some pillows, sheets and blankets in the hallway airing cupboard. He rocked Luke to sleep, laid him down in his travel cot and covered his little body with a pair of light frilly blankets. Then he got into bed alongside Pattie. The curtains were not properly closed and a shaft of street light fell across the far side of the room illuminating the chimney breast wall on which his mother's retirement gift of a sun clock still hung. He thought of the days when there had still been some sort of a family in this room and the latter days when his father had been weeping alone on the other side of the wall. He wondered what would happen to the new family that he belonged to now and whether it would end up any differently.

'What are you thinking about?' whispered Pattie.

He thought for a moment about how to put it, then shrugged.

'Just about the past. Sitting with my parents in this room. All those evenings when we read or watched TV or played games. And then hearing my father crying in his bedroom after my mother had died.'

'Aahh, I see...I think you need something to take your mind off all that.'

'You're probably right.'

'You really did look quite sexy today in your white shirt and black tie. And your haircut. Really smart...'

'Oh, no - not "smart" .'

'Not conveyor belt smart - individual smart. Cool smart.'

'Perhaps I should have been wearing dark glasses and smoking a Gauloise.'

'Dark glasses would have been enough.'

She pulled a sheath out of the packet beside the bed and swung it in front of his face.

'Are you sure these aren't past their use-by date?'

He smiled, then whispered:

'Put it on me.'

143

It was the first time they'd made love for two or three months and the climax was long and briefly obliterating. He lay on top of Pattie for a minute or so in the half-illuminated room talking and softly kissing. Then he sank back alongside her, probed with his finger until he found the magic button and slowly, doggedly, helped her to orgasm. He kept his arm around her for a while as a few soft tears flowed. Soon, both of them drifted into sleep and both were dragged out of sleep at 2am when Luke awoke crying. Pattie got out of the bed.

'Jesus,' groaned Will. 'Is there anybody who hasn't cried in this house - apart from me?'

'Your mother?'

'She cried once.'

He woke again three hours later, curled in the foetal position. He felt sure that he had been a child at home again in the last dream, but the detail was fading already. Daylight was filtering into the room and Luke was whimpering. Pattie stirred, half-opened her eyes and closed them again. Will got out of bed, put boxers and T-shirt on and went through the now-familiar routine, lifting his son out of the travel cot for a cuddle, laying him on the mat to change his nappy, leaning over him and all the while pulling funny faces and holding a one-way whispered conversation. Then he wrapped a blanket round him and carried him into the kitchen. He drew the curtains, took a bottle out of the fridge and heated it up in a bowl of warm water while still holding and rocking his son. When the milk was ready, he unlocked the back door and went into the garden. An old coal bunker jutted from the back of the bungalow and he perched on its wooden lid and fed Luke. Dew lay on the grass which was getting long again. Birds were singing and flitting to and fro in the slender young trees along fence lines. The orange light of the sun was starting to spread across the eastern sky. It was going to be another fine day, a good day. A song started up in his head, an old folk hymn that he'd heard on the radio once and never forgotten. He sang one of its verses soundlessly, lips moving as he retrieved each word and note from memory. He sang the next lines gently to Luke.

"Where are our dear fathers?
Oh where are our dear fathers?
They are gone to heaven shouting
Day is a-breaking in my soul'

144

'Of course, heaven is just a figure of speech,' he assured Luke who received this information stoically without blinking or letting his mouth slip from the rubber teat. Perhaps they should have played that song at the funeral? But everybody else would have been bemused. Nobody else would or could have shared his feelings. Not even Pattie. Had he done the right thing in having a graveside ceremony? Did it seem disrespectful, as if he had just wanted to get the event out of the way?

'I didn't mean it like that,' he said aloud. 'I just wanted to spare him from empty words. Even though he wouldn't have heard them.'

After a while though, he let the rest come out.

'I should have done more, shouldn't I Luke? I refused to accept bullshit, but what did we put in its place? Nothing much. No-one really commemorated him. I was the only person close to him, but I held back. I should at least have gone to see him in the Chapel of Rest.'

But the ceremony was over now and done with. No changes could be made. He saw the coffin again in the grave. Below it unseen in the earth was his mother's coffin. They were buried in the same place and that was it.

By this time, Luke had stopped sucking and Will gently took the bottle from his mouth and slipped it into his pocket. Then he stood and walked up the path to the far fence and back. Up he went and back again, over and over, with only the occasional pricking of little stones on bare feet to remind him where he was and what he was doing, until eventually Luke was winded and his baby eyes had closed. Thus he carried his son back into the silent house, not knowing then how much his father had meant to him for better or worse. Or how often he would dream of him in the years to come.